SOMETHING I SHOULD KNOW

SIOBHAN KALLI

Something I Should Know © Siobhan Kalli 2021

Printed and bound in the UK by
4edge, 22 Eldon Way, Hockley, Essex, SS5 4AD

ISBN: 978-1-913637-41-5

Published by
Candy Jar Books
Mackintosh House
136 Newport Road, Cardiff, CF24 1DJ, Wales, UK
www.candyjarbooks.co.uk

For Elise and Anton

I've lived with Mum all my life but I've never met my dad.

Never even seen a picture of him.

When I was little, Gran told me every family has its secrets. She called them skeletons in the cupboard. I knew she didn't mean real skeletons but, still, I always kept my wardrobe door wide open, so I could be sure there was nothing hiding in there, ready to jump out at me. Obviously, I was only a kid then. I realise now that it was just a metaphor to explain why families avoid talking about certain things, things that make them feel uncomfortable or embarrassed or ashamed.

Things like missing dads.

CHAPTER ONE

'That's ridiculous,' grumbles Mum, when I tell her about my homework assignment. 'I mean, what's the point?'

'Mr Lemone says family trees are an important part of social history,' I explain.

Mum unloads the dishwasher noisily and sighs. 'Well, I'll have to ask your gran if she can help.'

I should have known Mum would find a way to avoid talking about our family's past. On Saturday afternoon, she drops me off at Gran's house so I can look through the family albums.

'Your gran knows everything there is to know about the last three generations of Munroes,' Mum says, leaving me on the doorstep while she escapes to Pilates.

Gran ushers me in and I can see she's been busy. There are piles of photos and papers, certificates and letters, all laid out on the big table in the dining room. She loves talking about her family, growing up in Ireland, walking three miles to school every day, taking turns to collect buckets of water from the well and helping with the harvest in summer.

I help myself to the chocolate Hobnobs while she tells me about my great-great grandparents, her grandparents, her brothers and sisters. Soon I have everything I need, and we've sketched out the tree on a big piece of paper, and added in all the names, and she's even given me some grainy photos she says I can stick on, as long as I use Blu Tack and promise to give them back afterwards.

'Look at us, all as pale as milk bottles,' chuckles Gran, shaking her head at an old family snap of a beach holiday. There's Auntie Tash, Mum, Grandad and her lying on their beach towels, all squinting against the glare of the summer sun. 'We're all the same,' she adds. 'Can never get a tan.'

I look down at my bare arms, golden brown after a week with Mum in Majorca, and my heart skips a beat. I wait for Gran to realise what she's just said, but she's lost in reminiscing while I'm left with her words going round and round in my head. 'We're all the same…'

I gulp down my glass of milk and stare at the empty space on the family tree. My dad's side of the family.

'I can't give in my homework like that, Gran,' I say at last, sliding my palm across the white space. 'There must be something I can use. Do you have any pictures of… him?'

Gran's shoulders tense and she starts to gather up the paperwork and tidy away the photos. She seems to be in a rush.

2

'I've told you, love. I don't know anything about your dad. I never met him. Heaven forgive me, I'm ashamed to say it, but your mum really let us all down. Your grandad and I were so disappointed.'

I sink down into my chair. Gran always gets moody when my birth is mentioned. 'You mean *I* was a disappointment?'

She stops shuffling papers into a box file and takes both my hands in hers.

'No, no, *no*. You must never think that, Olivia. We were thrilled when you were born. You know how much we all love you. It's just that it was... awkward. You know what people are like. Asking questions. Talking behind your back.'

I picture Gran's friends from church, the silver-haired busy-bodies. It makes me angry to think of them gossiping about my mum. 'Look, Gran, I know you think people should be married before they have children, but one-parent families aren't that unusual these days.' Gran makes a little huffing sound and shakes her head.

'It's not just that, love. It's... it's... *you*. Having to grow up without a father. It's just not *right*. And now your Aunt Natasha's getting divorced, both my daughters are single parents. Poor little Charlotte's going to grow up without her dad, too. Where did I go wrong?'

Gran puts her head in her hands and looks as if she's about to cry. I stand up and put my arms around her. Looking up at me, she pats my cheek

3

gently. 'We must have faith, sweetheart. You know what they say, every rainbow has a silver lining.'

'You mean 'every cloud…?''

Gran cuts me off, 'I know what I mean! Don't you worry, my darling.' She points to the ceiling and leans towards me close enough for me to hear her whisper: 'It's all part of His plan, you know.' I nod my head, more from habit than agreement. It's a comforting thought, I suppose. But it won't help me with my homework.

CHAPTER TWO

When I get home, I find Mum in the kitchen. I unroll the sheet of paper and lay it down on the worktop, right under her nose.

'My family tree. What do you think, Mum?'

She glances at it and carries on peeling carrots. 'Looks good, Ollie. Did you find everything you needed?'

'You haven't even looked at it properly! And no – duh! If you *had* looked, you'd have seen a massive space on my dad's side. *Obviously.*'

'Oh.'

'Yes, *'oh'*. So what am I going to do? I can't hand in my homework like this.'

Mum shakes her head. 'That teacher, did he not stop to think about what sort of problems this would create?' She puts down the carrots and peeler and turns towards me. I'm sorry, Ollie. I really am. But I can't help you.'

Fury sends heat to my cheeks and sets my heart galloping. 'Can't help me? *Can't help me?* Everyone has a father. Even if he was a donor from a sperm bank. So what's the big secret, Mum?'

'Trust me, Ollie. I'm just trying to do what's best for you.'

'But I have a right to know!' I shoot back, not even caring that I'm shouting now.

Mum swallows and tucks a few loose strands of hair behind her ear. 'I've told you before: when you're older, I'll explain everything. But you're a child and I just want you to grow up safe and happy and…'

'Well, I'm not happy, Mum. And I won't be until you tell me the truth! And I'm not exactly a child any more, I'm thirteen. I'm a *teenager*, Mum…' Then something occurs to me, mid-rant.

I take a breath and lower my voice. 'Did something bad happen to you, Mum? Is that it? Did my dad hurt you?'

Mum looks horrified. 'No! No way! It wasn't like that. Me and your dad, we loved each other. It just didn't work out.' She sighs. 'It's… complicated.'

'It's okay, Mum, I can take "complicated". I'm old enough to understand. I really want to know. *Please!*'

Taking a step closer, she tries to give me a hug. I step backwards out of reach.

There's something else I need to ask. 'Mum, do you remember those letters I used to write to him?' Mum looks at me warily.

The first time I wrote to my dad was just before my seventh birthday. While Mum was writing out the invitations to my party, I asked if I could send him one, too. I wrote:

Dear Dad,
Do you know you have a daughter?
Do you know my address?
Would you like to come to my birthday party?

Of course, he didn't come. But I still remember the excitement of thinking that he might. One day. After that, I sent him a Christmas card. And a Father's Day card. Easter cards. At school, when we made cards to take home to our families for special occasions, I would always make two, an extra one for him. I'd given all the letters and cards to Mum, so she could post them to my dad.

Eventually, I'd stopped writing to him, when it became obvious he was never going to reply.

'Why do you think he never wrote back, Mum?' I wait for her to answer but I already know what she's going to say from the look on her face. 'You didn't send them to him, did you?'

She shakes her head and looks at the floor instead of at me. 'I couldn't, sweetheart. Because I don't know where he lives.'

'So, what *did* you do with them?' My voice quivers on the edge of anger.

Mum bites her bottom lip. 'I've still got them.'

It's such a relief to get an honest answer from her, for a second I forget she's been lying to me for the past six years. Lying about every piece of paper and card, each and every envelope I had sealed with a kiss and a lick of spit and a dream of my dad's happy face when he would open it up and read my messages. 'So, where are they?' I'm amazed at how patient I sound, like a weary parent trying to squeeze the truth out of a naughty child.

She clears her throat. 'In a shoebox at the back of my wardrobe.'

Even though I'd kind of expected her to say something like this, a dull, heavy ache crash-lands in my chest. Why hadn't she just thrown them away? Would that have been any worse than deceiving me all this time?

I swallow. 'Okay. Can I have them back, please?'

I shut myself in my bedroom and open the box. There are so many envelopes in there, all different sizes and colours, all addressed to 'Dad' in swirly felt tip and decorated with hearts and flowers. All those messages of love to a person I'd never met. Fat tears spill down my cheeks. What am I going to do now? I pick up my phone and text Charlie:

Can you come over?

I add a crying emoji.

CHAPTER THREE

'That's ridiculous,' says Charlie, pulling a tissue from the box on the bed and handing it to me. I blow my nose again. 'Listen, Ol. You're a teenager now, not a kid. You totally have a right to know who your biological father is.' My cousin Charlie is my best friend. We're the same age, well, I'm forty-three days older, and we've always been like sisters.

'I know,' I sniff. 'But Mum says I'm not old enough to understand.'

Charlie's mouth moves sideways and she does her 'thinking' face. 'Maybe you don't have to wait for your mum to tell you.' I sense a lightbulb moment. Yep, here it comes. Her eyes open wider and she starts flapping her hands. 'Oh my God, Ol, I've just had the most amazing idea. I totally know how we can find your dad. You know that show, *Find Your Family*?'

I frown, wondering if she's finally lost the plot, while she opens my laptop and taps the keys impatiently. Charlie binge-watches reality TV. Her favourite's that one where they sit by the pool all summer, crying and arguing about who fancies who. And, lately, she's become obsessed with the one where people try to find the perfect wedding dress. I think it's something do with Auntie Tash and Uncle Joe splitting up.

I've watched *Find Your Family* a couple of times. It's the one where they reunite family members who've lost touch. She turns the screen around to show me. 'Look. This is Frank. He never knew his mum and then one day he gets a phone call out of the blue and BOOM! Next thing, he's on the show and they've flown him all the way to Canada to meet the woman who gave birth to him and had to put him up for adoption.' When she clicks 'play' on the screen, we watch the final minutes of the episode, where a middle-aged man in shorts, t-shirt and socks-under-sandals, is introduced to a grey-haired woman in a powder-blue trouser suit and purple flowery scarf. They hug and kiss and say how much they've thought about each other every day and how they can't wait to meet all the other relatives and make up for lost time. Then they cry and laugh and, by the end, even the presenters are crying and laughing, and the audience is clapping as the credits roll. Charlie looks at me proudly and presses 'pause'.

'See? Easy!'

She can't be serious. 'Are you actually saying I should apply to go on a reality TV show?'

'Why not? If it's the only way?'

I shake my head, thinking of all the reasons why this wouldn't work. 'For a start, Mum wouldn't agree to it.'

Charlie shuts the laptop and puts it down on the bed. 'It's what I would do if I were you. I don't know how you can stand not knowing,' she says, linking her fingers round a bunch of her long, silky hair, pulling it over her shoulder and starting to work the strands into a fishtail braid.

She's right about that. It's the secrecy I hate. But there's still the problem of persuading Mum. 'What if she says no?'

'If you're that worried, don't tell her. Not yet. Then, if you do get chosen to be on the show, it'll be too late for her to stop you. And if she tries, you call Childline. Or you take her to court and say your Human Rights have been violated!' Charlie has a habit of getting herself all worked up about a new cause. Last week, it was animal testing by the cosmetics industry. She threw all her make-up out and made her mum buy her the cruelty-free versions instead.

I know she's determined to get me to agree. And, already, a tiny part of me is secretly starting to like this mad idea of hers. Maybe I should go along with it and see what happens. Another thought is still nagging me, though.

'But... suppose *he* doesn't want to meet *me*?'

Charlie puts her hands on my shoulders and grips me fiercely. 'Listen to me. You are his

11

daughter. You are awesome. Of course he'll totally want to meet you.' But would he? Really? I'm not so sure, but my cousin's eyes sparkle with confidence. And glitter eye shadow. 'Look, remember Frank? He's old and bald and he's got wonky teeth but his mum's blissed that she's finally found him. He's her child. She's his parent. It's the strongest bond in the world!'

I can't help smiling, imagining the scene. Me, running into my dad's arms. Him, beaming with happiness to have found me. And I'd finally get the answers to all my questions. A bubble of excitement floats up from somewhere under my ribs.

Charlie's excited too. She keeps bouncing up and down on my bed and asking if she can come with me when they do the filming and all the interviews and everything. She might be getting a bit carried away about being on a TV show but at least she's enthusiastic. 'Ooooh, and can I do your hair and make-up? You could *so* do with a makeover, no offence.'

I stare at my cousin's biscuit-brown foundation and mascara-thick lashes. Make-up's not really my thing. 'Yes, yes, of course you can,' I say with a nod. 'But will you stop bouncing – you're making me feel sick!' Charlie kneels behind me and starts to French-braid a handful of my wild, curly hair. Okay. But only if you let me play hairdressers.'

I love my cousin. She's always on my side. But can I trust her? 'Seriously, though. I need to think it over first, Charlie. And you can't mention it to anybody, not yet. If Mum finds out and she says no, I might have lost my chance to find my dad.' Just saying the words 'find my dad' gives me a fizzy feeling in my stomach.

'Don't worry, Ol. You know I can totally keep a secret. This will just be between you and me.'

'Swear?'

'Swear.'

'Blood swear?'

'Blood swear.'

Instantly, I relax. When we Blood Swear, we mean it. It's our thing. We've told each other loads of secrets over the years and kept our promises to each other. Of course I can trust Charlie. We're a team. Together, we're going to find my dad.

Mum taps on the door and pops her head round. 'You two okay in here?' We nod frantically, looking as innocent as possible. 'Charlie, your mum's coming to pick you up. Something about dance practice?'

'I'll text you later,' I say. Charlie picks up her bag and mouths 'check the website' over her shoulder on her way out.

CHAPTER FOUR

I've got Maths homework to finish and then I find a French verbs worksheet I'd forgotten about. It's getting late when I finally open the website for *Find Your Family*. A wave of excitement surges through me as I click on 'Application Process'. They want the basic background story, any information that might help them with their search, and there's a form to fill in. They want to know why you would like to meet that family member and what it would mean to you.

I download the forms and start reading. Right at the end, there's a sentence that nearly stops me from breathing.

'Applicants must be over twenty-one'.

How could I have been so stupid?

There it is in black and white. I don't know whether to cry or scream. I'm annoyed with myself *and* with Charlie. I shouldn't have let myself get carried away like that. I hammer my fists on the mattress and let hot tears run down my cheeks.

I'd got my hopes up for nothing and now I'd have to forget the whole thing. I pick up my mobile and call Charlie.

'What is it?' she yawns. 'Have you been on the website yet?'

'Yes, I have,' I croak, wiping my tears with the back of my hand. 'And there's a slight problem. Check the "Terms and Conditions".' I wait as she taps at the keys on her laptop. 'See? It's right at the bottom of the page.'

'Okay, got it. Oh, right. Yeah, you have to be over twenty-one.'

I roll my eyes. 'Tell me something I *don't* know.'

'But that's not a problem…'

I'm suddenly furious at how chilled she's acting. 'What, you mean I should just wait another eight years? That's easy for you to say, you've got a dad!' My cheeks are burning with rage and fear, not to mention embarrassment at my own stupidity.

'Whoah, calm down, Ol. I'm totally on your side here. Look, it's simple.' I hold my breath and wait to hear what she's going to come up with. 'We put your mum's name on the form, not yours.'

'*What*? Are you insane?' I don't know whether to laugh or tell her to get lost and forget her stupid idea. 'She'd never agree to it.' My voice cracks and I pinch my lips together, determined not to start crying again.

'Who says we have to tell her?' Charlie's question sounds light and easy and full of possibility. And ridiculous. And impossible.

And, maybe, brilliant.

CHAPTER FIVE

'What did you tell your mum?'

'*Nothing*, Ol. Don't worry. I just said I need photos of me as a baby for Art homework.

We're sitting on Charlie's top bunk, legs crossed, with a stack of clear Perspex boxes in front of us. These are the photos that didn't make it into Auntie Tash's glossy albums. Most of the pictures are ones where Mum's not camera-ready or Auntie Tash's hair's not perfect. Some have captions written on the back: 'Charlotte and Olivia's first day at school' and 'First Prize on World Book Day' where I'm dressed as *The Diary of a Wimpy Kid*, actually *dressed as the diary*, not one of the characters. Mum made that costume out of a cardboard box nearly as big as me. She'd got her paints out and copied the front cover of the book in perfect detail. It had shoulder straps attached, so I could step right into the box and walk around in it.

Things have been weird with Mum since she handed over the box of letters. She keeps asking me if I'm okay and trying to hug me and I can tell she feels guilty. I made her write me a note for Mr Lemone saying sorry I couldn't complete my History homework due to unforeseen circumstances. Obviously a lie. Whenever I feel guilty about keeping my mission to find my dad a secret, I remind myself that lying doesn't seem to bother Mum that much when it suits her. The most difficult part of the whole thing is remembering to act like I'm still angry with her when really I'm so excited about *Find Your Family* I can't think of anything else and I lie awake at night imagining the day I finally get to meet my dad.

We're looking for pictures that might have been taken when my mum was with him, maybe on a night out or a holiday or a party. Anything. Mum says she doesn't have any pictures of him but I don't believe her. Who doesn't have a picture of a boyfriend they made a baby with?

I find one of me and my cousin at Junior Gymnastics club. We used to look quite similar back then, small and chubby with round cheeks. But now she's turning into this glamorous, skinny, cat-walk model with long, blonde hair and I've got curves everywhere and dark hair, even on my arms, and she's so cool and I've got a hot temper that keeps getting me into trouble. Charlie looks like her mum and my mum looks like her mum did when she was young. I'm the one that looks different. If you took a picture of me and Charlie now, standing side by side, dressed in leotards, you wouldn't even think we're related.

I really want a picture of my dad. Do I look like him?

'Check this out,' Charlie says, handing me a small close-up of two heads bent towards each other. It's her mum and dad, on their wedding day. They look totally in love. I search her face for clues to how she feels about this. She never talks about her mum and dad splitting up. She avoids mentioning her dad at all and I know she's always finding excuses not to see him when he makes plans to take her out at the weekends.

'Cute,' I say with a smile, handing it back to her. She sticks out her tongue at the couple in the picture and flops backwards onto a pile of cushions. I flop backwards too, and we lie with our heads touching. 'Charlie, we've spent ages looking through these and there's nothing here. What next?' I stare at the ceiling, thinking, while Charlie picks up her phone and scrolls through YouTube videos.

'We're going to have to do some sleuthing, Ol, that's what. If we can't find the evidence we need, we're going to have to start thinking like detectives.'

'Okay, Sherlock. I get it. But where do we start?'

She puts down her phone and rolls over onto her front. 'Well, let's see what we need. Did you print off the application form?'

I pull a sheet of paper from my bag and smooth it out on the duvet.

Charlie runs her finger down the form. 'Okay,

first thing is, *"Name of the person you are trying to find"*.

'*Doh!*' we say at the same time.

Charlie swings her hair around and it hits me in the face. 'Like, if we knew that, it would be easy. We could just Google him up, *et voila*!' Charlie's been using a lot of French words since she did *her* family tree and found out one of her great-grandparents on her dad's side was from Paris. That's History homework for you. 'Hey, do you think your dad might be from another country? That would explain why your mum doesn't know where he lives. Maybe they had a holiday romance. *Ooh, la la!*'

'Maybe,' I shrug. Whenever anyone at school asks me awkward questions about my dad, I always tell them he lives a long way away.

'So, we're going to have to get a name, for a start. Are you sure your mum's never mentioned your dad's name, Ol?'

'Er, I think I would have remembered!' Stupid question. And I've seen my birth certificate. The space for the father's name was left blank.

'Okay, no need to get sarcastic. Hang on, though. Don't you think *my* mum must know his name?'

'Oh, *yeah*.' There's no way Mum would have kept her boyfriend a secret from her sister.

'Right, I'll get on to that. What else does the form ask for? *"Approximate Age: (if known)"*.'

'How are we going to find that out?'

'We don't need to. We can guess. Let's say he's about your mum's age, yeah?'

'I suppose. What else?'

'It asks for "*Relationship of the person to you*" so that's easy. We put "Ex-boyfriend and father of my child".'

My insides flip over when I imagine Mum finding out what we've done. I'm not comfortable with keeping secrets, but I remind myself I have no choice. I mean, if she won't tell me, what else can I do? I need to know who my dad is. *It's something I should know.* Charlie carries on reading:

'They want to know "*What were the circumstances of your separation?*" We can make something up. Something dramatic that will get us, I mean your mum, I mean you, on the show. How about, "a tragic misunderstanding" – do you think that will grab their interest? Or do you think it has to be more specific? How about "We were torn apart by family circumstances"?

I don't know what to say because I don't know what I think. Suddenly, I feel the enthusiasm draining out of me. I look at Charlie, all perky and excited and try to feel the same.

'Do you really think this is going to work?' I sigh. I know I must sound ungrateful. Charlie is putting in all this effort to help me. I wish I could be more upbeat, like her. But I can't help it. What if it all comes to nothing? What if we can't find him or, even worse, what if we do and he doesn't want to have anything to do with me?

CHAPTER SIX

My phone buzzes and I read my cousin's text.

> Bingo! Prepare to be astounded at my genius, Holmes. Coming over now. Xx

She only lives ten minutes' walk away but by the time Charlie arrives, I'm a wreck. I'm all sweaty and my heart is doing weird fluttery things and my hands are shaky.

She bursts through the bedroom door, gasping, and puts her hands on her knees while she catches her breath.

I'm ready to wet myself with impatience. 'What is it? What have you found?'

Charlie straightens up and takes a deep breath. 'Your dad,' she breathes, 'I know where he met your mum. They were students at the same uni.'

I nod, trying to remember the last time Mum talked about her student days. A few years ago, she went to the wedding of someone off her university course. I remember because she'd stayed overnight so I'd had a sleepover at Charlie's. We'd watched a film about vampires and we were so terrified we'd stayed awake all night. I don't remember Mum saying much about her old friends from uni or talking about the wedding much, but to be fair I hadn't really asked, probably because I was too tired.

'How did you find out? Did you ask your mum?'

'No, my dad told me. He didn't have a choice. I said I needed to know and he owed me the truth after walking out on me and Mum, and I made him feel so guilty he came out with it. I think he's worried though. He wanted to know why I was asking and I said it was for a school project on genetics.'

'But you're not genetically related to my dad.'

'*Obviously*. But by the time he'd worked that out, it was too late. He said to keep it to myself, though. Apparently, your mum goes mad if anyone even mentions it.'

'So, what's next, I mean, what can we do now? To find him.'

Charlie sits down on my bed and I sit beside her.

'Well, it's a start, but it's not enough,' she admits. 'What we really need is a name.'

'Right. If we have a name, we have enough information to fill out the form.' I look at Charlie and I can see she's thinking the same thing.

'Your mum needs to tell you, Ol. But if she won't, we're going to have to do everything we can to find it ourselves.'

CHAPTER SEVEN

Charlie and I are with Uncle Joe, queuing for our cinema tickets, and I'm starting to wonder if it was a good idea to agree to join them. Charlie begged me to come along and I could hardly say no, with her helping with finding my dad and everything, even though the film's a Pixar animation and sounds a bit babyish to me. But she's been in a proper mood ever since she got in the car.

I know she's annoyed that she always has to go out somewhere when her dad wants to see her; he's been sleeping on a friend's sofa since he moved out of their house. He's made it clear that as soon as he sorts out a place of his own, there'll be a spare room for Charlie so she can come over whenever she likes. But, for now at least, they have to make do with meeting elsewhere and that makes Charlie furious. It's sad because she used to get on so well with her dad. And he's always been really nice to me, as if he was trying to make up for me not having a dad of my own around. But now it's just awkward. Even though I don't have anything to be angry at him about, it's like I have to go along with Charlie and act as if I do.

'Look, if you're hungry I'll get you some popcorn,' offers my uncle. Charlie folds her arms and turns away. She won't even look at him. 'I just don't feel comfortable eating at Macdonald's, Charlie. You know how I feel about it. All that meat, all that packaging. It's not healthy and it's not good for the planet.'

'Mum always lets me have a burger when we come here,' Charlie snaps, though she's still refusing to look at him. She's staring across the car park at the big yellow 'M' and all the people happily rushing in for their Happy Meals and rushing out even more happily with their brown paper bags full of the kind of food her dad hates. She swings around all of a sudden, furious that she's not getting her way. I shuffle my feet and wonder when my cousin turned so angry. She never used to be like this. I didn't even think she liked burgers that much. She said they made her spotty.

'Just because you're a vegan doesn't mean we all have to be, you know!' she snarls though gritted teeth. 'Mum says I can eat whatever I want!'

Uncle Joe shrugs. 'Of course you can eat what you want. Just not fast food, please. That's all I'm asking. Besides, I'm sure your mum would like you to eat something more healthy.'

He's so calm and reasonable, I can tell Charlie's

finding it difficult to think of an angry response. After racking her brains for a few moments, she manages to come up with, 'This film looks dumb. I'll have some toffee popcorn, though. Might die of starvation otherwise.'

Uncle Joe turns to me as we shuffle along the queue. 'Same for you, Ollie?'

I nod. 'Yes, please.' Charlie glares at me as if being polite to her dad is a sign of disloyalty. I don't know what she's blaming me for. It was her idea for us to get together. She's convinced he knows more than he's let on about the identity of my dad and she's determined to squeeze it out of him. I'm not sure if being a brat is going to help, though. Charlie nudges me gently with her elbow and frowns. 'Sorry, you know what I'm like when I get *hangry.'*

For the next hour and twenty-five minutes, we sit in silence in the dark, crunching our way through our bags of popcorn. The film's not even that bad. Afterwards, Uncle Joe offers to take us to a vegan café run by a friend of his on the other side of town and Charlie agrees without so much as a curl of her glossy upper lip.

She seems to quickly forget about her resentment and switches into full-on interrogation mode. She's not even subtle.

'I want you to tell us everything you know about Ollie's dad,' she orders, shovelling a veggie burger into her mouth. 'Mmm. This is not actually that bad,' she nods, licking ketchup from the corner of her mouth. Uncle Joe coughs and looks like he's going to choke on his marinated tofu and has to take a gulp of water quickly.

'What? Where did that come from? Look, I've told you everything I know,' he says, looking at me uneasily. 'Why all this sudden interest, anyway? Ollie? Has your mum told you anything more about him?'

I feel my face burning. 'No… no. She hasn't. She says she'll tell me when I'm older.'

Uncle Joe tips his head to the side. 'Well, if that's what she says, I'm afraid we have to respect her wishes,' he says softly. 'Sorry.'

'But it's not fair!' Charlie blurts out, putting what's left of the burger down on her plate. She's already demolished half of it. So much for her loyalty to the Big Mac. 'Everyone needs to know who their father is. Ollie's got a right to know!'

I'm touched by my cousin's support. I'm so lucky to have her on my side. She has a knack of being very persuasive. I look at my uncle and wonder what he's going to say. He shrugs. 'I've already put my foot in it, telling you they were on the same course at uni. I'll get in so much trouble if your mum finds out.'

I look at my cousin. Her eyebrow twitches but she avoids my eyes. I know she's thinking what I'm thinking. 'On the *same course* at uni.' That's what he said. New information. This could be the breakthrough we'd been waiting for. Surely there can't have been that many people on the same course?

'So that's it, you're not going to help Ollie, then?' she accuses, fake-sulking. Uncle Joe shrugs and says nothing. We finish our meal in silence.

On the car ride home, Charlie picks a fight with her dad about driving a car and polluting the planet. I'm not sure if he actually agrees with her or is just winding her up but he says he's been thinking of selling it and next time he takes her out he'll make sure they use sustainable means of transport. Like the bus. She ignores him after that and starts texting me instead.

So your mum and dad were on the same course at uni.

I know! Do you think that's going to help us find him?

Yup! It's another clue. We just need a name now. Lucky my dad's such a bigmouth. Maybe there's more he can tell us.

Poor Uncle Joe's going to be in trouble if Mum ever finds out he let that slip. But I have to stop worrying about everyone else's feelings. This is about me.

CHAPTER EIGHT

Auntie Tash bustles in and Charlie plods sheepishly behind her. 'I told her not to wear that crop-top but she wouldn't listen.' My auntie launches into full-on harassed-mum mode while my cousin stands behind her, rolling her eyes.

Mum can't respond because she's nose-to-nose with the hallway mirror, applying mascara with the concentration of a brain surgeon.

'There's nothing wrong with it,' sighs Charlie, tugging at the elastic and pulling it down towards the top of her leggings.

'It's okay for the beach,' humphs my auntie.

Charlie looks at me for back-up, but I can't think of anything to say because she always looks great. 'It's a statement piece,' she explains.

'Really?' her mum asks, but it doesn't sound like a question.

'I knew you wouldn't understand,' Charlie mumbles.

'Oh, I understand. That top's a statement piece, all right. The statement it's making is "I'm cold, put some clothes over me!"' she says, making her voice go squeaky.

'You're not funny, you know. Tell her, Auntie Em,' Charlie appeals to Mum as a last resort.

Mum puts the mascara back in her make-up bag and looks Charlie up and down. 'I think you look lovely, sweetheart.'

My auntie looks furious. She can be quite fierce when she's angry. Let's just say she doesn't like to be contradicted. I always thought Uncle Joe was a little bit afraid of her. When he'd told her he wanted to become a vegan, she went mad and said he had to choose between a life with her or his hippy-dippy nonsense. To everyone's amazement, he chose his hippy-dippy nonsense.

'Oh, I give up.' Auntie Tash looks at her watch. 'Shouldn't your gran be here by now?'

A silhouette appears behind the glass in the front door and the bell rings.

'There she is. Like clockwork.' Mum laughs, and Gran comes in and kisses each of us in turn and gets her slippers out of her coat pocket.

'Make yourself comfortable, Mum,' Auntie Tash says, winking at me. She's cheered up a bit already. She loves going out and she looks really glamorous, as usual, in high heels, a shimmery silver dress and matching handbag. 'Look after your gran, won't you, girls.'

'We will,' we chorus.

'Isn't it supposed to be the other way around?' smiles Gran, easing herself into an armchair and pulling out a pile of magazines from her vast shopping bag.

'Would you like a cup of tea, Gran?' Charlie offers while I push the footstool nearer to Gran's feet.

'Oooh, I feel like royalty,' she says with a laugh, flicking through the crossword magazine. 'Now, come and help me with this. I got stuck on this one. A seven-letter word for legal division.'

Mum slips on her coat. She looks really pretty. I've hardly ever seen her look so dressed up, apart from her office's Christmas party or the odd family wedding. She's straightened her hair so it's all silky and she's wearing this gorgeous black dress with red roses all over it and cherry-red lipstick that really suits her. She looks so young and alive and… not like a mum.

'Wow!' I breathe. 'You look amazing, Mum.'

Gran nods approvingly. 'You're a good-looking pair, there's no doubt about that.'

'Taxi's here,' shouts my auntie. They clip-clop out of the front door and we wave them off. Charlie makes Gran a cup of tea and brings it in on a tray.

'Divorce,' Charlie announces.

'Eh?' I frown.

'That's your seven-letter word, Gran.'

'Oh yes. Clever girl. But aren't you cold in that little top?'

'No, I'm fine, Gran. Don't worry about me. Shall we finish the crossword together?' Charlie looks at me and lifts her eyebrows as far as they'll go. That's the signal. She pulls up a chair next to Gran's and I sneak upstairs.

It was my idea to wait until Mum goes out and do some investigating in her absence. Now though, my heart's beating really fast and my hands are shaking as I open up her wardrobe and wonder where to start. It's a huge antique monster of a thing. It was a great hide-and-seek place when we were little and once Charlie got really scared when she shut herself in by accident; she'd been reading *The Lion, the Witch and the Wardrobe* and was convinced she was going to fall out of the back of it into another world and get captured by a witch.

As well as being stuffed with clothes, there are boxes stacked up on the floor of the wardrobe, more boxes stacked up on the top shelves and even storage boxes sitting on the very top of the thing. Charlie's convinced that somewhere in here is the evidence we need. A name. My dad's name. It makes sense. There's not much storage space in our two-bedroomed house and Mum must keep all our certificates and papers and documents here. I can't think of anywhere else they could be.

I get down on my knees and pull out a small cardboard box. It's got my old baby things in it: my first pair of soft shoes, my name-tag from the hospital where I was born, a tiny silver bangle and a cross and chain. I put the lid back on, put it to one side and pull out another box. This one's full of my old swimming and gymnastics badges and rosettes for races I'd won on sports day. There are school photos of me at different ages, too, all the way through from Nursery to Year Six. I shake my head at the state of my hair, in various states of hideousness, from wild curly bush to full-on bird's nest. Maybe Charlie's right about me needing a makeover. I put that aside, too, making sure to remember where these boxes were, so I can replace them when I've finished. There are folders and files. I flick through them – one's got old gas and electricity and water bills, one's full of bank, credit card and council tax statements. I get quicker at opening folders and putting them back. Soon I've been through almost everything.

There are a few more folders right at the back, under some shoe boxes and I pull one out. It's big and flat and inside are Mum's certificates for music and her GCSEs, all her school reports (I'd *love* to read these, but there's no time now), her university papers, listing the courses she took and an old prospectus for the University of Leeds. I pick up a stiff, cardboard envelope and slide out a thick piece of paper embossed with a crest and printed in fancy swirly letters. It's her degree certificate. It reads: 'Archaeology and Anthropology, First Class Honours'. Wow – I never knew Mum got a first-class degree. Isn't that the highest score you can get? There's something else in the envelope and I carefully ease it out. It's the programme for the graduation ceremony. It's got all the names of the students who graduated the same time as Mum. *All the names*.

'Olivia, are you all right up there?' Gran's voice floats up from the bottom of the stairs.

'Yeah, fine, Gran. Nearly finished.' I frantically start to put the boxes back where they were, beads of sweat breaking out on my forehead, hoping my cousin can keep Gran safely out of the way. If Gran burst in, I don't know how I'd explain snooping through my mum's private papers and I didn't fancy trying. I shove the programme underneath the wardrobe and jog down the stairs.

'I promised Mum I'd give my room a bit of a tidy. Charlie doesn't want to sleep in a pigsty,' I tell her, hoping my red face doesn't give me away. I feel so guilty. I guess I'm not cut out for lying. But when I think about what's sitting under Mum's wardrobe, I can't help feeling excited. Charlie meets my eye and she can tell I've found something. I just need her to go and get it and put it somewhere safe.

'Gran, can you show me how to do Sudoku again? I say sweetly, swapping places with Charlie.

'Just popping to the loo,' Charlie says, while I mouth 'under the wardrobe' as Gran turn the pages to the 'easy' section of her Sudoku puzzle book and starts to patiently explain that's it's all about the numbers one to nine. 'And each number can only appear once in a line or in a square…'

I'm so excited I can hardly breathe but I try to

stay calm and focus on the numbers, nodding as Gran starts to fill in the boxes with her biro.

Later, when we've finished watching a show Gran loves about people who buy ugly ornaments from junk shops and try to sell them for profit at an auction, and Gran starts to look like she's going to nod off, Charlie and I kiss her on the cheek and say goodnight, even though it's only nine-thirty.

'Night-night, girls. That's right, now, you get your beauty sleep.'

We run up the stairs and I can't wait. 'Where did you put it?' I hiss. Charlie pulls the programme out from under my pillow. 'It's right here.'

'Did you get a chance to look at it?'

'I had a quick scan. There are about fifteen names on the same course as her. Five women and ten men.'

'So, one of them's my dad!'

'Yup, guess so. Except—'

'What?' I feel the blood in my veins turn colder. 'Except what, Charlie?'

'It's just that, we don't know for sure they finished the course in the same year. He could have been older than your mum. Or younger.'

'Meaning?'

'Meaning he might not be on the list of names of students who graduated the same year as your mum.'

'Oh, right.' I feel my body go limp. This is so exhausting, all this excitement, building up hope, then being disappointed again. 'But how can we find that out?'

Charlie unpacks her pyjamas and toothbrush from her bag and frowns. 'I'm not sure yet. But don't worry, Ol. I'll think of something.'

When she goes to the bathroom, I pick up the programme and read through the list of names. They all sound ordinary, there's an Andrew and a James and a Peter. There's one that stands out. Alexandros Papadopoulos. I wonder if he's from a different country. That's quite an unusual name.

I hear a car pulling up outside. 'They're back. Quick, turn that light off,' I tell Charlie. She flicks the switch, shoves the laptop under my bed and settles down on the pull-out. We listen as someone fumbles with a key and hear Mum and Auntie Tash giggle and tell each other to 'shush' and hear Gran waking up and saying her goodbyes as they bustle her into the taxi.

I put the programme under my pillow for safe-keeping. I'll put it back in the wardrobe as soon as I get a chance.

CHAPTER NINE

Mum and Auntie Tash sound like they're having a row. Charlie pulls on a sweatshirt and spends ages side-plaiting a chunk of her hair, then undoing it again. 'Bet they're hungover,' she says, pulling a face. 'I think it's disgusting, going out and getting drunk, at their age.'

'I don't think I've even seen my mum drunk, or with a hangover,' I say, staring at the printed pages of the University of Leeds Graduation Programme. I can't take my eyes off it. It's as if I expect my dad's name to come to life, leap off the page and shake my hand.

We hear a raised voice. It's my auntie's. She sounds angry. 'I'm free to go out with anyone I want! In case you haven't noticed, I am now a single woman.' I can't hear what my mum says because she's keeping her voice down. This sounds like it's an argument Charlie and I aren't supposed to hear. Charlie goes to the door and opens it a crack. Her mum's angry tones float up the stairs. 'Well I like him. He's taking me out tonight. To the fancy new place run by that chef off the TV. Apparently, it's always booked up months in advance but Bernard knows the *maître d* so we'll get VIP treatment.'

'Are you sure he's your type?' Mum asks. There's a note of defiance in her question. She doesn't normally dare to contradict my auntie. Not many people do.

'Of course he's my type,' my aunt replies, sounding exasperated. 'He's rich, good-looking and he knows how to spoil a girl. *Unlike* my ex!' Charlie flinches and I wonder if we should shut the door and put on some music. It's horrible hearing her mum say negative things about her dad. Charlie opens the door wide enough so her head's sticking out. Part of me wants to put my fingers in my ears so I don't have to hear this and the other part of me is burning with curiosity. I expect Charlie feels the same. I can't believe my auntie's got a boyfriend!

'I'm just saying, maybe you should take it slowly. You don't know anything about him yet.' My mum sounds weary. Once my auntie starts on you, you can't get away from her unless you agree with whatever it is she's saying. My mum knows this better than anyone.

'You know your trouble, don't you,' Auntie Tash says, her voice rough and snarly. 'You can't get over that Greek guy. What was his name again? Oh, give me a minute. Adonis, wasn't it? The Greek god of love?' She cackles at her own joke.

'It's not funny,' Mum says sadly. 'He was the love of my life.'

'Hah – yeah! And where did that get you? Bringing up a kid on your own. Don't talk to me about love! Love doesn't walk away from a child and just disappear!'

'You don't know the whole story,' Mum says, keeping her voice even. I can tell she's not far from crying. But I don't think that's going to stop my aunt. Not now she's on a roll.

'No, because you keep it all to yourself. I don't know why you're protecting him. He was a loser. He let you down. And Ollie. Maybe we both chose duds. Well, I don't want to be a sad single for the rest of my life. I want Charlie to have a man around, a real one.'

Mum mumbles something that we can't hear. Next thing, Auntie Tash is shouting up the stairs and we quickly shut the bedroom door so she doesn't know we've been spying. 'Charlie! Get your stuff. We're going!' I give Charlie a quick hug and she picks up her bag. I hear the front door slam.

They didn't even stay for breakfast.

CHAPTER TEN

There was only one name on that graduation programme that stood out. My fingers tremble as I pick it up and I stare at it, the name. *His* name. It's a real name. He's a real person. I knew that before, obviously, but now that I can see it in black and white it's as though this person has transformed from something vague and imagined to someone living and breathing, somewhere in a far-off country. I run my finger over the printed letters.

It only takes ten minutes for Charlie to Skype me. I knew she'd be bursting to talk so I've got my laptop open and ready. Her face fills the screen and her eyes are wide with excitement. Before I can speak, she says exactly what I'm about to say. It's all I've been able to think about since she and my auntie left in such a hurry. I've been sitting on my bed, numb with shock, trying to take in the news. My dad was Greek. *Is Greek.* My chest feels like it's going to burst and I have to remind myself to breathe. 'He's Greek! Your dad! You're half Greek, Ol.'

'I know!' I gasp. Greek! *Greek!* Oh my God. I feel different already. My dark hair makes sense now, and the way I tan easily while Mum just burns after ten minutes in the sun, or just gets more freckles. I try to imagine the country my dad comes from, Greece. I think of ancient Greek temples, mythological Gods with superpowers and sunny holidays by the sea. Jade from netball went to a Greek island last year; she showed me some pictures on her phone and it looked amazing – all blue sky and perfect beaches and these cute little white houses. Mum said Greece was too hot when I told her I really fancied going there. We go to Spain every summer instead, which is scorching hot, too, come to think of it. Now it makes sense, though. She's avoiding the place that reminds her of my dad.

Except none of it makes any sense, at all.

Why avoid him when she said he was the love of her life?

Charlie's playing some music on her phone and she turns it up loud so I can hear, then she stands up and holds out her arms. She starts clicking her fingers and then she does this weird thing with her leg. Oh I get it. Greek dancing. I saw this in a film once. I stand up and join in and we kick our legs in time with the music and laugh.

I'm still fizzing with excitement. I'm Greek! Now I feel sure I'm going to meet my dad for the first time.

Charlie is the first to stop and she sits down in front of the screen again. 'What was that name on the programme again, Ol?'

'Alexandros Papadopoulos.'

Charlie repeats each syllable slowly and carefully. 'That definitely sounds like a Greek name. Let me Google it to check.'

I could have done that already if I hadn't been frozen into a state of shock.

I hold my breath and wait.

'Yep, it's Greek. Hah – typical. It says here it's the most common surname in Greece. *Lol*! Like, you're the Greek equivalent of a 'Smith', Ol!'

I blink and look at Charlie and she looks at me and I can tell we've just had the same thought.

'You know what this means, Ol?'

I nod. 'We've got a name. We can fill in the form and send it off to *Find Your Family*.'

'Totally right. OMG, do you know what I've just realised? It's just like *Mamma Mia*! You know, you're like Sophie, trying to find her dad?' I'm still lost in thought and can't think of a suitable reply. 'Or maybe it's more a like *Mamma Mia* backwards. 'Cos you'll be going to Greece to find him, not the other way round. Are you listening, Ol?'

Now that it's really happening, the old fears start to come back. Suddenly my stomach feels hollow and my blood goes cold.

Charlie instantly reads my change of mood. 'What's wrong, Ol? I thought you'd be happy...'

'I am happy. It's what I wanted, what I want. It's just... I feel a bit scared.'

'Scared? Of what? You're going to meet your dad at last.'

'I *know*. I can't explain it. Maybe it's… maybe it's just that I've got used to things the way they are and now I'm going to have to get used to something completely different.'

'What's wrong with that? You're not happy without your dad. You'll be better off finding out who he is, what happened, why he disappeared off the scene. You've always said it was the not knowing that you hated.'

I give a long and heavy sigh. 'Yeah, you're right. I'm going to have to face telling Mum, though. I'm not sure I'm ready for that.'

'There's no hurry, Ol,' Charlie says, in her most soothing voice. 'Take your time. It's a lot to take in.'

Charlie uses her knack of knowing how to calm me down. I feel the pressure lifting and I smile a 'thank you' in her direction.

'But… while you're getting used to the idea, we could fill in the form and send it off. It might take ages for them to reply. I bet they have to read through hundreds of applications.'

I shake my head. 'No, I'm not ready for that yet, Charlie. I need to get used to the idea first. *And* I need to find a way to tell Mum. Just leave it for a bit, yeah?'

'Of course,' my cousin says softly. 'Just let me know when you're ready, okay? I'll be right here, and remember, I'm on your side. We can tell your mum together if it helps.'

'Thanks, I might need you with me when the time comes.'

CHAPTER ELEVEN

The thing about Mum is she's so transparent. I'm busy stacking the dishwasher after Sunday lunch when she decides this would be a good time to initiate peace talks.

We've been avoiding each other for weeks now; I'm still annoyed with her about the family tree and the secrets and the lying. We've barely spoken about anything other than everyday stuff like what I want for tea and if I've done my homework. I know she feels bad and I hate it when we fall out. Usually one of us will sulk for a bit, then eventually say sorry. But I'm known for my stubbornness and this time there's just no way I can forgive her. So, when she tells me out of the blue that she's going to leave work early tomorrow so she can pick me up from school and we can go out for our tea, I know exactly what she's up to. What's more, she thinks catching me off-guard gives her the upper hand.

I carry on stacking the dishwasher, biding my time, determined not to give her the reaction she wants. Breathe, slowly, in... out... I need to think carefully before I speak. If I get annoyed she'll look like the innocent victim and I'll look like the villain. She's the one who's in the wrong and I need to keep reminding myself of that. I wait to hear what she's going to say; in my head, I'm predicting her exact words. If it's 'we could do with a bit of quality time together', I swear I will scream.

'I just thought we could do with a bit of qual… some time together. It's been ages.'

I bite my lip and swallow. It's so obvious she's trying to force us into one of her 'little chats'. The thing, is, she doesn't know I overheard her argument with Auntie Tash. What would she say if I told her I know my dad is someone she met at uni, he's Greek and, what's more, I even know his name? I could force her to tell me the whole story. How can I let her carry on keeping a secret when it's not a secret anymore? I imagine telling her and making her face up to the past. But something's stopping me. I don't want to force her into it. There'll only be a row. Finding out who my dad is should be something special, not something that becomes known because of a row or in the middle of a shouting match. The thought makes me shudder. I want to know but I want her to *want* to tell me. Why does everything have to be so difficult and complicated?

In the end I shrug and say 'Okay,' quietly, avoiding her gaze.

*

I join the waves of kids pushing through the main doors, most of them clearly nothing short of desperate to get out of school. I see Mum's car across the road and she gives me a little wave. I get in, answer her predictable questions about my day – who I sat with at lunch and whether I've got homework or not – as briefly as possible. Once we've parked, jogged across the road through a sudden shower and been shown to our table in Luigi's Pizza Place, she looks at me over the top of the menu.

'Shall we order the usual?' The waiter comes over and she tells him exactly what we want in one breathless sentence: 'Hi, two Cokes please, and we'll have the garlic bread and the breaded mushrooms to start, then the four seasons thin crust for me and the Mediterranean thin and crispy for my daughter, thanksverymuch.'

She's forgotten I always have extra olives on the side; I'm tempted to ask for them but change my mind. I'm curious as to how she's going to play this and I'm going to let her do the talking.

When the waiter's gone to get our drinks, Mum clasps her hands together and rests them on the table. She takes a breath and I can't help feeling a bit sorry for her. I'm still annoyed but it's clear she's struggling with this, too.

'So, Olivia, it's time we had an honest chat,' she smiles, a little awkwardly.

Hah! Honest? Really? I fold my arms and lean

back in my seat, leaving a silence to fill the space between us. She sighs and carries on.

'I've been thinking. And… you're right. There are things I should tell you and you are old enough to know who your dad was. Is.'

I do a quick double-take. This is not what I was expecting. There's a mad flapping in my chest, like a bird trying to escape from a locked cage. The waiter's back, plonking glasses down on the table between us and we wait in silence for him leave us in peace.

Mum leans forward and lays a hand on my arm. I look up and for the first time it's clear to me how sad the whole situation is and how hard it is for her, how hard it's always been for her. I think of all the years that have gone by, her doing her best as a single parent. This wasn't how she'd wanted things to work out. She never set out to have a baby and bring it up on her own. But she's always put me first. I gulp and swallow. We lock eyes and I give her a little smile of encouragement. I want her to know I'm not angry with her any more. Then she starts to talk.

She tells me about my dad, his name, Alexandros, how they met at uni and were friends for years, but how he disappeared for months at the end of the summer term in their final year, coming back just in time for the final exams. She never did find out why he'd gone away, but she'd always suspected there was something he wasn't telling her. He didn't tell any of their friends, either, because she'd asked around at the time but no one had heard from him. Then, when he'd returned out of the blue, they were all so wrapped up in their exams, there wasn't much time for socialising or catching up so it wasn't until their last week as students that she'd had a chance to talk to him properly. Some of their friends had already left to start summer jobs but they'd both decided to stay on until after the graduation ceremony. Without the distraction of studying, with most of their friends gone, they'd started spending more and more of their time together.

'It was a magical time,' Mum sighs, blinking away the tears. 'I... we... well, I suppose you could say, we fell in love.' She blushes and places her hands down on the table. With a gentle giggle, she gets that faraway look as she remembers how it all started and begins to tell me the story. 'It was almost as if we'd just met for the first time. We were in our own little love bubble.' I do a cringe face – I can't help it – then apologise immediately, for fear that she won't carry on with the story, but she doesn't miss a beat. 'We were like tourists, spending our days sunbathing in the city park, visiting the sights and the galleries we'd never got round to bothering with before. It was lovely, like a little holiday.' She stops and pinches her lips together. 'Maybe that's all it was. A holiday romance.'

'What do you mean? It can't have been. You were already friends. It was more than a holiday romance. It had to be.' I stop talking for fear of sounding ridiculous. I mean, if anyone knows about the relationship, it's my mum. She doesn't need her daughter to teen-splain it to her. All the same, I know there's more she's not saying. I hold my tongue and wait, even though I'm desperate to hear what she's going to say.

She nods. 'Yes, that's what I told myself. But maybe I got it wrong. Otherwise, why would he have refused to speak to me ever again?'

My eyes goggle in disbelief. I feel sure she must have got it wrong. There must have been some misunderstanding. 'What did he actually say? How did he…?' I can't even form the right questions. My mouth goes dry and I try to imagine what was going through my dad's head when he dropped my mum like a stone after a whirlwind romance. Of course, it's impossible to understand his reasons. I don't even know him and even Mum couldn't make sense of it, so what chance do I have? Maybe there are more clues, though. Maybe Mum did something to put him off, though I can't imagine what that could have been. Was someone else involved? Did he meet someone he liked better? I don't want to say it because it sounds too hurtful. I expect Mum's considered that possibility anyway.

'Anyway,' Mum carries on. 'None of that matters right now. I want you to know who your father is. I thought about what you said and you're right: it is something you should know. So I tracked down Rob, an old friend of his I bumped into at that wedding a few years back. I thought he still might still be in touch with him, and Rob said he might be able to get an address for Alex.'

I'm stunned. She's finally done it. Mum's taken my demand to meet my dad seriously. Even though it must have been so difficult for her. And it's risky – we don't know what we'll find out.

As if she's reading my mind, Mum says, 'Of course, I can't make any promises. He may not be able to find him. And even if he does…'

'It's okay, Mum. I know. He might run a mile when he finds out he's a dad.'

'I wasn't going to say that, love. But you're right to… manage your expectations, shall we say.'

I nod, thinking about the roller-coaster of feelings I've had in the last few weeks, from excitement to disappointment to disbelief to fear and now… well, more fear. I'm not sure how I should feel about all this. Yes, I still want to find my dad, of course I do, but the thought of all the build-up, and the hoping, and the excitement of finally meeting him; then the thought of the chance of disappointment. Can something be unbearable and exciting at the same time?

'But I think we should try,' Mum continues. 'And now's as good a time as any.'

I want to tell her about what I already know,

and I know I should confess to my snooping around behind her back, but something stops me. I just can't. She'd hate me, even more than I hate myself at this moment. I feel so bad, the way I've been deceiving her. Should I speak up now, and get it over with? I open my mouth and try to form the words to explain what Charlie and I have been up to. But I can't do it. How could I have snooped on my own mum? I'm a terrible daughter. I must have been frowning because Mum notices something's bothering me and, thinking she knows what's wrong, she apologises, saying, 'Hey – I nearly forgot!', catching the waiter's eye. He skips over to our table. 'Can I get a side-order of olives for my daughter, please?' He nods and comes back quickly with a tiny plate of glistening black olives swimming in olive oil.

'You didn't think I'd forget your favourites, did you?' she smiles.

I remind myself that at least we didn't get as far as sending off the form to *Find Your Family*. We can just put the whole thing behind us. I know I can trust Charlie to keep quiet about it.

CHAPTER TWELVE

We stop by Charlie and Auntie Tash's house on the way home. Well, I do. Things are still pretty frosty between my mum and my auntie so she waves at her sister from a safe distance, then drives off. Charlie's been off school with a cold so I agreed to drop off some notes she needed for Geography homework. I find her in her bedroom, lying on top of her duvet, zipped up into her Scooby Doo onesie, looking miserable. I'm dying to tell her about Mum's revelations but before I can get a word in, she launches into a rant about her dad, who'd been round earlier to pick up the last of his clothes.

'You won't believe it, Ol. He's says he's left his job at the bank and he was taking all his suits to the charity shop on the High Street because he won't need them anymore. He lives in his old jeans and faded t-shirts now *and* he's growing a beard and – his *hair*! It'll be long enough for a ponytail soon. He's turning into a completely new person. And, get this – he's moved in with Al, that guy who owns the vegan café and he's going to help him do up his house instead of paying rent. He asked me if I wanted to go on a protest march about climate change but Mum said I'm too young. Still treating me like a baby! I was so annoyed at her I told Dad I'd love to go, even though it sounds boring. And anyway, what good will a stupid old march do?' She finally pauses for breath, plucking a tissue from a box of mansize by the bed and blowing her nose noisily.

'You look terrible,' I tell her, passing her the bin. It's evidently the wrong thing to say, because she promptly bursts into a fresh eruption of sobs. It's not the cold; I doubt she's even ill. I know my cousin. She's having a meltdown. It's all the more shocking because it's such a rare event. She's usually the one doing the comforting. I put my arm around her and she sobs into my shoulder. 'It's okay,' I soothe her. I'd been kind of wondering when this would happen. I knew it wasn't natural to be so cool about your parents splitting up. 'It's okay to be sad. It must be hard now he's finally moved all his stuff out.' Even I find it hard to believe Uncle Joe's not living there anymore. Charlie throws a bunch of tissues in the bin and wipes her eyes on her sleeves. 'It's not just that,' she sniffs, her voice thick with tears. 'It's Mum. I saw her with that guy we heard her and your mum talking about. I was on the bus on the way home from netball club on Monday and there they were, walking along the street. And they were holding hands! And laughing together, just like that couple off the telly…'

'Which couple?' I frown, trying to picture what's in Charlie's head.

'You know, in that advert, the one where they're running along the beach, laughing, with the wind throwing their hair around.'

'Not the advert for the yoghurt with the good bacteria!?'

'Exactly! That's the one!' says my cousin, jabbing the air with her finger.

'Who knew bacteria could make people so happy!' I giggle. Suddenly, we're both laughing. My cousin's snapped out of her momentary meltdown and she's more like her old self.

'I must look a sight,' she snorts, snatching a hand mirror off her bedside table. 'Oh no, my nose. It's bright red and swollen.'

'Put some concealer on it, it'll be fine,' I say, passing her the tube.

She sighs and smiles and it's nice to see her relax again.

'Everything's changing, Ol. Dad's gone, Mum's moved on – oh God. What if she gets married again and I have to live with a stepdad!' I take her hand before she starts getting herself worked up again. 'Whoa, slow down. You don't even know how things are going to go with your mum and this new guy. It might just be a fling. Or a … what do they call it, rebound thing.'

Nodding, Charlie chews over my words and we sit in silence.

Maybe we're both thinking about how important our dads are in our lives. I open my mouth, desperate to tell her what Mum told me.

My phone buzzes. 'Mum. She says it's time I went home.' I text her back: *'coming now'*. I can't believe I'm not going to be able to tell Charlie my news straight away. If I want to tell her in person, it'll have to wait. 'I'll come over tomorrow. There's stuff I have to tell you,' I say, giving her a quick hug and shrugging my parka back on.

'Mum, is it okay if we have our tea early? And can we have a pizza? And can we eat in the kitchen, so we can get on with our project afterwards? Ollie can only stay for a couple of hours.'

To my surprise, Auntie Tash nods her agreement. She's normally so strict about eating together in the dining room, the table all set with napkins that match the china, even on a school night. I suppose now it's just the two of them, she's not so bothered about keeping up the old routine. There's something else that's different about my auntie, though. And I'm pretty sure it's to do with this new man in her life. I can't exactly ask Charlie about it, though. She's still super sensitive about her mum having a boyfriend and has a habit of doing vomiting mimes every time the name 'Bernard' is mentioned.

The only thing I know about him is that his name's pronounced 'Ber-naaard', to rhyme with 'regard', like he's French or something, even though Auntie Tash said he's from somewhere in Yorkshire. The first time my cousin met him was when Auntie Tash invited him over for dinner. All she'd told me about him was that he'd asked her what school she went to and what subjects she liked and what her hobbies were. It sounded like he didn't know much about kids because he asked her if she was doing her GCSEs this year even though she'd told him she was only in Year Eight. 'And he thought netball was like lacrosse so I explained it's more like basketball except you can't bounce the ball and that we don't play lacrosse at our school,' she added with a smirk.

Surprisingly, Charlie didn't seem to hate him on first sight, as I'd been expecting. She mimicked his posh voice and took the mickey a bit: 'He said "absolutely, absolutely" a lot and stroked his moustache when he was talking. Then he told me about all the countries he'd visited when he was in the army and to be honest I got a bit bored, but Mum seems happy so that's the main thing.' Then, she finally paused for breath and asked, 'Anyway, tell me what's new with you?'

CHAPTER THIRTEEN

Before she even speaks, I pick up a vibe from Mum. It's like static, an atmospheric crackle in the air. She's sitting at the kitchen table with her glasses on the end of her nose, looking up at me, eyes like searchlights.

'I got a really weird email today,' she announces in a voice that's calm but with undertones of something else – menace maybe? I plonk my bag down on the kitchen table and slip off my shoes.

'From who? School?' I grab a cookie and take a big bite, scanning my brain for anything I've done that might have got me into trouble. 'If it's about the detention, it wasn't just me. The whole class got told to stay behind…'

'No, not from school,' she interrupts. Her eyes glint and I recognise that look. I'm in trouble. Whatever it is, it's got my nerves jumping. The clump of cookie suddenly feels as dry as cotton wool in my mouth and I freeze, waiting and still wondering what I've done wrong. Mum turns her laptop round so I can see the screen. I lean forward and start to read. It's a letter. There's a logo in the corner and before I even twig what's going on, the words start dancing before my disbelieving eyes, and then there's the lightbulb moment. I only have to skim over the words 'application', 'Greek', 'child' and *Find Your Family* and a cold rush sweeps through my veins.

Could what I think has happened actually have happened? Is it possible Charlie sent the application off after all? *Even though I told her not to?*

'It's… I'm sorry. I c… can explain,' I stammer.

'Good. I was hoping you'd say that. Because I need someone to explain to me why I've been invited to appear on a reality TV show to… how did they put it again… "reconnect with an important person from my past"?'

Her voice is getting gradually louder and there's a pink flush to her cheeks and neck. Mum rarely gets angry. I don't know what to do. This wasn't supposed to happen. Especially now that she's opened up to me. She put her trust in me and it looks like I've betrayed her. I put my head in my hands. I can't meet the look of disappointment in her eyes. I want to tell her this is all Charlie's fault but I don't because that wouldn't be fair. Because it wasn't all her fault at all. I went along with it; we were in this thing together. She senses I'm hiding something and I want to tell her everything. But where do I start?

'Did someone put you up to this?' she asks,

tapping her finger on her chin. Was it my sister, your auntie Tash? Was this all her idea?' I can tell how furious Mum is just imagining that was the case.

'No! No, it wasn't Auntie Tash. It was my idea and, well, Charlie helped…'

'Ah, Charlie,' she interrupts,' I might have known. That girl's always up to something.'

'Oh come on, Mum. You know that's not true.'

'Isn't it? Well, let's get her over here now and she can tell me herself what she was thinking when she, or both of you, decided to impersonate me and apply to a reality TV show in my name. Do you know this counts as identity fraud?'

The tears start to flow before she's finished her sentence, but she ignores my despair and jabs at the buttons on her phone. 'They're coming over now, both Auntie Tash and Charlie. And when they do, you can tell them what a ridiculous idea it was. I mean, can you imagine? Me? Take part in a lame TV show? As if.'

CHAPTER FOURTEEN

I stare out of the window at the city skyline behind the 'Pandora Productions' logo stencilled onto the glass wall in front of us.

Ros, the producer, is swivelling from side to side in her sleek leather-and-chrome desk chair. 'It's going to make great TV,' she says, looking round at the faces of the people gathered at the table, but giving the impression that she's talking to herself. She turns to me. 'It's going to mean a lot for you to find your dad,' she nods over at Mum, 'and your ex, isn't it?'

Mark, the researcher, leans forward. 'It'll be like *Mamma Mia* but in real life!'

Ros ignores him. 'You must both be curious about meeting him, and perhaps a little anxious too. All perfectly normal emotions.'

'That's what we do best. Emotions...' nods Mark, grinning enthusiastically.

'Of course, Ros continues, 'It's not quite to formula... what I mean is, it's not like the usual stories we do, about adoption and families being separated through tragic family circumstances.

Still, I think we've got a great story here and we think our viewers will love it!'

'How do you feel about meeting your dad at last?' Mark asks, tipping his head to one side and fiddling with his silver earring.

'Ratings will go through the roof!' announces Ros, looking at the ceiling.

'We'll try our best to ease you through the process and keep you informed of what's happening at every stage of the show. We also have counsellors at hand to talk you through the emotional side of things.' Mark crosses his palms over his chest as he says the word 'emotional'. 'I promise, we'll take it slowly.'

'Can you imagine the press coverage?' Ros is still talking to herself out loud. 'We've never had a show like this. Are you both happy to travel to Greece?' I look at Mum and nod, and she nods back at Ros.

'Ah, Greece. What a fabulous backdrop. This might even win us a TV Gold Award. I can't tell you how excited I am. You people have no idea what a big deal this is… I mean, what a great show this is going to be—'

'So, on the practical side,' Mark interrupts firmly but still using his kind-and-caring voice, 'we think we've found a contact who knows where Alexandros is living.' He pushes a piece of paper across the table. Mum and I peer at the pictures of whitewashed houses with narrow cobbled streets, washed in sunshine, under a bright blue sky. A road sign in Greek and English reads '*Παραμύθι - Paramithi*'.

Mum's on the edge of her seat. 'Yes, that's it. I remember him telling me. That's the name of his family's village. *Paramithi*. Is he living there?'

Mark coughs gently. 'We think so. There are quite a few people with the name Alexandros Papadopoulos. It's quite a common name, actually. But we think we may have found him.' He leans forward and looks at me kindly. 'I know what a big deal this is for you. I didn't get to meet my dad until I was twenty-one. We want to get this right.'

I nod and swallow, thinking of all the warnings from Mum about not getting carried away and remembering to be realistic and 'manage my expectations'. It was all very well saying those things and I really wanted to *try* to follow their advice, but, like, how could I not be really, really excited right now? These were experts, they'd reunited hundreds of families live on national TV, and now it was my turn. I was sure they'd found my dad, or if they hadn't yet, they would. And if he wanted to appear on the show, that meant he wanted to meet Mum and put things straight. 'Does he know about me?' I ask, swallowing down more anxiety. Mark and Ros exchange a look. 'Not exactly,' Mark answers. 'Like I said, we want to be sure everything is in place first. The last thing we'd want is to put you through all this for nothing.' That word 'nothing' has an instant effect: I feel my bubble of excitement deflating, the hope leaking out of my pores. Mum squeezes my hand and gives me an encouraging smile. I know what she's thinking. We've come this far…

Ros stands up, to show the meeting is over. She holds out her hand and, as Mum shakes it, Ros gabbles on about how Mark will be in touch once they've confirmed contracts and will of course send us detailed schedules and full travel itineraries as well as our fee.

I say 'bye' to Mark. He hands me the sheet of paper with the pictures of Paramithi and I slip it into my rucksack before we say our goodbyes and step through the shiny doors and into to lift that takes us back down the fourteen floors to the Reception area. Then we push our way through the revolving glass doors and out onto the busy pavement.

Charlie, Auntie Tash and Bernard are sitting in a posh café across the road. We wait for a gap in the busy traffic, then jog across, narrowly missing being mown down by a cyclist who comes out of nowhere.

Mum launches herself through the doors of the café and we flop down in the empty seats at my cousin's table.

Auntie Tash is beside herself with excitement. 'Well, come on, then. Tell us what happened?'

Before Mum can reply, Bernard chips in, 'Take

your time, Emily. There's no rush. Let's all remember to have a little decorum.' He clicks his fingers at a waiter and orders Mum a double macchiato and me a Diet Coke even though I'm pretty sure Mum usually drinks skinny lattes and I avoid any drink with the word 'diet' before it since I learned about artificial sweeteners in a Biology lesson. Auntie Tash rolls her eyes impatiently. Everyone else is just amazed at what Bernard can get away with. My auntie's in awe of him and seems happy to let him boss her about. Gran said that's what the first flush of love does to you. Charlie seems to think he's okay, but that might be because he keeps buying her stuff. Yesterday, he presented her with a brand new iPhone, which explains why she's busy swiping through all its features and has barely noticed me or Mum since we came in.

Mum looks round the table and grins. 'They think they've found him, Alexandros.'

My auntie squeals then stops abruptly when Bernard sends her a look; he has this way of making his face into a kind of sideways frown. It's funny but disturbing at the same time. She does a dainty cough and asks in a polite voice: 'What do you mean "think"? Have they found him or not?'

Mum sighs. 'It seems they have. They've got to do some more research, some checks, just to be sure. Apparently, Alexandros Papadopoulos is a very common name in Greece.'

'Told you, Ol. You're like the Greek equivalent of "Smith",' chimes in my cousin, without looking up. I'm quite pleased when everyone ignores her and my mum carries on. 'They're going to let us know when things are finalised. Then, if all goes to plan, we'll get a schedule for filming. They're going to fly us out to Greece to film the reunion!' There are more squeals from my auntie and Bernard lets out a loud laugh that sounds a bit like a horse whinnying. And, at last, Charlie looks up, her face coming alive with more excitement than I've seen in her for ages. 'Who's flying to Greece? Can we all come?'

'Actually, they mentioned that we're allowed to take two extra family members with us, for emotional support.'

'Yup, they're big on emotional support…' I nod.

Mum explains, 'I haven't had a chance to think about who we should take with us. Do you think maybe your gran would like to join us?' she asks, turning to me. I nod, thinking how much Gran would love a trip to Greece and a chance to be on a TV show. Not to mention finally meeting my mysterious dad and putting an end to the gossip for good. 'So that leaves one more person we can take.' We look at Charlie, then at Auntie Tash and at Bernard. This looks like it's going to be one of those awkward moments. For once, I'm glad Bernard is there. He comes up with a plan straight away.

'Of course, you should go, Charlotte. You two came up with this whole plan in the first place.' She eyes him suspiciously and I know what she's thinking: is it an excuse to get rid of her for a few days, a week maybe, and have Auntie Tash all to himself? But he surprises everyone by announcing, 'Your mother and I will come along too, but we'll pay our own way. If that's all right with everyone?' No one can think of an objection. Auntie Tash seems happy with the suggestion. I knew there was no way she'd let an opportunity like this slip past her.

Mum hugs her sister. 'That's fabulous. I was so hoping you'd come. I didn't want to leave you out, but they only offered to pay for two family members and I knew you wouldn't want to come without Bernard.'

'So that's all sorted then. Who's going to tell your gran?' asks Bernard.

'I know. How about we break the news at her birthday party? We should have confirmation by then. We might even be able to present her with the tickets – can you imagine how surprised she's going to be?' says Mum.

'Yes! Great idea. She'll be thrilled. Who wouldn't want a week in the sun? And she's always complaining about the cold…' says Auntie Tash.

Bernard has a faraway look in his eyes. 'It'll be just like "*Mamma Mia*",' he says, turning to my auntie with a soppy look on his face.

I *wish* people would stop saying that.

CHAPTER FIFTEEN

We've assembled in the living room, the whole family, even Bernard, everyone squashed in, watching Gran opening her birthday presents. There are 'oohs' and 'ahhs' and 'oh, lovely, another scarf' and 'this is so kind of you all, you know, you needn't have bothered'. The only person who's not here is Uncle Joe, who'd said he might be a bit late. Everyone's so excited; to be honest I think we've all forgotten he was even coming, because by the time somebody notices, we've already sung 'Happy Birthday' and Gran has cut the cake.

'Just one more present,' says Mum mysteriously. There's a stillness in the room as we all hold our breath, waiting for Gran to open the envelope. She slides her forefinger under the seal and makes a tear, which she widens by inching her finger under the fold, painfully slowly. After about a century, she slides a sheet of paper out and unfolds it.

'What's this?' her voice is high-pitched with surprise as her eyes scan the details printed on the ticket.

'It's a ticket, Gran. A plane ticket to Greece,' Auntie Tash explains.

'I don't understand. Why would I want to go to Greece on my own?'

Mum takes Gran's hand and sits her down gently on the sofa. 'We've got a surprise for you. It's about Olivia's dad. You always said you wanted to know who he was. Well, now you're going to get a chance to meet him!'

Auntie Tash can hardly keep still; she's so desperate to tell the story, she butts in before Mum can finish. 'We're off to Greece, Mum. We're going to be on a TV show and everything!' As the words tumble out of my auntie's mouth in a flurry of news about emails, researchers, a friend from university, the father of Emily's child, we all freeze, watching Gran's expression as the information soaks in. She says nothing, sitting still and poised, her lips pressed together. I know that look. There's a long silence.

'What on earth are you all talking about?' she asks, shaking her head. 'Is this some kind of joke? Why would I want to go to Greece? And what's this about Olivia's father?' She turns the full force of her gaze on Mum. 'I thought you said he was dead!'

Mum breathes in a horrified gasp and looks at me, then back at Gran. 'I never said that, Mum. I said…'

'You as good as said it. You let us all think that there was no way you'd ever see him again.'

'I may have said he was... dead to me. But's that's just an expression. It was in the heat of the moment. I don't think you realise what a devastating time it was...'

'Always so secretive. Not a word to me or your poor dad, no explanation at all. I don't know how you thought this would work out, without people getting hurt. Especially your poor daughter. You can't run away from the truth, you know.'

'Well, I'm not running away, am I? Not anymore. That's why we're going to Greece...'

'Well, good luck to you to. To *all* of you. But I'll tell you this...' Gran looks around to make sure she's got an audience, picks up the ticket and tears it in half, then in half again. She tears and tears until it's in little bits, which she throws up into the air. We all stand and stare as the shreds of paper float through the air like confetti. 'I won't be going with you!'

Mum covers her face with her hands, flops sideways onto the sofa and curls herself up into a ball. Charlie puts her arm round me and gently pulls me out of the room. We run up to my bedroom and shut the door. I can't hold the tears in any longer and start to sob. She wraps an arm around my heaving shoulders.

'I'm so sorry, Ol. This is totally my fault. If I hadn't—'

'No!' I sniff, wiping my eyes on my sleeves. 'Don't say that. None of this is your fault. I'm the one who wanted to meet my dad.'

'What do you mean, "wanted" to? You do still want to meet him, don't you?' Instead of sounding relieved, as I'd expected, Charlie's voice has a hint of panic. Or is it anger?

I blow my nose loudly into a tissue and look at Charlie. Is that what she's really worried about, that she'll miss out on a free holiday and a chance to be on a TV show?

Is that all this is to her? Does she even care about my feelings at all?

I think about how she sent off the form to the TV company behind my back. Was that really her trying to help me? Or was she being selfish? Oh, I just don't know who I can trust any more. Before I can take my disappointment out on her, though, there's a little tap on the door and Gran walks in. She sends Charlie a 'look'; Charlie nods and slips silently out of the room, shutting the door behind her. Gran sits down next to me on the edge of the bed and takes my hand in both of hers.

'Olivia, my darling. Don't be crying, now. You're disappointed. I know. Your mother should never have done this. Getting you all excited. It's not right.'

'It's not Mum's fault,' I sigh, shaking my head.

'Well, I don't know about that…'

I can't bear to listen to Gran's criticisms of Mum, not again. I've had enough. I stand up. 'Gran, you've got to stop this. This isn't about what you or your church friends think. This is about me wanting to know who I am. Wait. I've got something to show you.'

I open my wardrobe and, reaching up on my tiptoes, I carefully take down the shoebox with all my letters and cards to my dad. 'Look. See for yourself. I've wanted to meet my dad for as long as I can remember.' I place the box on Gran's lap and lift off the lid. She starts to run her fingers through the pile of cards, picks up letters at random and scans them in disbelief. She reads everything, all the cards, the messages, the invitations. Finally, she looks up at me with watery eyes.

'Oh, love. Come here.' She hugs me close. 'You can take them to Greece and give them to your dad at last!'

'Do you think he'll be happy to meet me, though, Gran? How do we know he won't freak out when he finds out he's got a daughter? What about… if... he…'

'Now, now,' she soothes. 'We'll jump off that bridge when we get to it.'

'Don't you mean "cross" that bridge?' I ask.

Gran ignores me and stands up, smoothing down her smart dress, the one she always wears to parties. 'Come on, now. Let's go and tell your mum.'

Charlie's been lurking about outside my door; when we come out, she takes one look at us and races me to the bottom of the stairs, while Gran follows at a more sensible speed behind us.

'Can you print out another ticket? Looks like we're off to Greece!' I shout, before pushing the living room door open and nearly knocking Uncle Joe over in my hurry to beat Charlie.

'Whoa, slow down, you two,' he laughs, helping me back up on to my feet. 'So, what have I missed? And what's all this about going to Greece?'

CHAPTER SIXTEEN

'So what did your dad say about you going on a trip to Greece? And your mum and Bernard coming too. I mean, was he jealous or anything?' I'm in my room, watching Charlie show off the contents of her shopping bags. She picks up yet another cool bikini with matching shorts, sarong and flip-flops. Bernard took her and Auntie Tash on a massive shopping trip and I watch bewildered and a little bit jealous while she shows off her fabulous holiday wardrobe.

Charlie shakes her head and flings handfuls of clothes into the open mouth of the huge suitcase on the bed. 'He was totally chill. You know what he's like about his carbon footprint and everything, so it's not like he'd have come anyway.' She grabs another carrier bag and upends it, scattering yet more new summer clothes across the duvet.

I can't believe she's suddenly okay with Bernard being with her mum now. She doesn't even seem to be worried about getting a 'new dad' any more. Even though they haven't announced anything yet, it's pretty clear Auntie Tash and Bernard are serious about each other. And going on holiday is taking things to the next stage. Is that all it took to get on Charlie's good side, a few new outfits?

'You know we're only going to be staying for a week, don't you?' I frown, wondering if I need to remind my cousin that this trip is about *me finding my dad*, not her having a free holiday. We still haven't talked about how she broke her promise and sent off the form to *Find Your Family* when I'd asked her to wait until I was ready. I'd always trusted her and then she went behind my back.

'*Yeess*, I do know. And what a fabulous week it's going to be,' Charlie sighs, draping a floaty maxi dress across her and studying her reflection in the full-length mirror. 'Imagine. Our whole family on a TV show. We're going to be famous!'

Her breezy mood annoys me. As if this is about being famous! That's the last thing on my mind. Sometimes my cousin is so self-obsessed. She should be helping *me* to prepare for this huge event, the biggest thing that's ever happened to me, not worrying about how she's going to look.

'You know I'm still mad at you. You shouldn't have sent off the form without telling me.' My cheeks burn when I think of the deceit. 'I feel like I can't trust anyone in this family…'

Charlie's shoulders droop. She lets the dress fall onto the bed and flops down next to the open suitcase.

'I'm just excited, that's all. Sorry if I got carried

away,' she says quietly.

'I know,' I sigh. 'I'm excited too. But I'm also really scared. There's so much to think about. My whole life is about to change.'

'Er, *yeah*. Change for the better, remember? And about the form. You're right. I shouldn't have sent it off. But it all worked out for the best, didn't it? You know all I want is for you to find your dad at last and be happy, don't you?'

I shrug. But I know she's right. It did all work out for the best. So what's the point of staying mad at her?

Charlie senses the shift in my mood and smiles. 'Sooo... have you decided what you're going to wear for the big day? You know, when you finally get to meet him?' She kneels on the bed and starts to sift through my pile of clothes. I'd tried on just about everything I owned but nothing seemed to look quite right.

'No, I need help,' I admit. I'd been hoping Charlie would give me the benefit of her style expertise. She picks up a short pink dress with a lacey bodice and net skirt. Mum had bought it for me last year to wear to her friend's baby's christening. 'Nah, too "prom queen",' she announces, throwing it on the floor. Next, she grabs a series of tops and skirts, sighing loudly and adding them to the 'no' pile. 'Oh, dear. Looks like your mum needs to take you shopping,' she sighs at last, the entire contents of my wardrobe rejected and lying in a heap by my feet.

I shake my head. 'Mum says there's no money for new clothes. She's had to take unpaid time off work for the trip. We'll get a fee for being on the show, but that won't come through until after we've finished filming.'

Charlie shakes her head disapprovingly. 'Hasn't your mum heard of credit cards?' she says with a tut. She thinks for a few seconds, then the lightbulb moment happens. She rummages in a bag and pulls out a sliver of blue material. It's silky and light and shimmers in different shades of turquoise and sky blue, like a swimming pool glittering in the sunshine. 'This is perfect,' she decides. 'Try it on!' I try to persuade her I can't. I'm sure it won't fit. But she slips it over my head, over my t-shirt and jeans, and turns me round to face the mirror.

'Wow,' I breathe. Even with my clothes underneath, it looks amazing. And it does fit. It's not even tight. It's floaty and gorgeous and has little spaghetti straps on the shoulders. And it must be made of some kind of magic material that flatters my curves and brings out the blue in my eyes. 'Are you sure I don't look like a Kardashian?' I frown, twisting round to check how my bum looks.

Charlie smiles and shakes her head. She lifts up a handful of my hair and curls it into a bun. 'There. That's the look we want. Greek goddess meets English rose.' Something's sticking in to my shoulder; it's the price tag. I look at it and let out a whistle. 'No way. I can't borrow this. It's brand new *and* it cost a fortune.'

'Don't be silly. You have to wear it. It's perfect. And don't worry about the money. If Bernard wants to fling his cash about, it's fine by me.'

All the same, it doesn't feel right. 'Are you sure? I mean, what will Bernard and your mum say? Don't you think we should ask them first?' Charlie shakes her head and looks away. 'You leave those two to me,' she says, picking up a brush and sliding it through my wild curls. 'Now, let's play hairdressers.'

CHAPTER SEVENTEEN

Mum taps lightly on my bedroom door. 'All packed and ready?' she asks, hovering in the doorway. I'm sitting on my bed, my laptop on my knees, and even without looking up from the screen I can read her body language and I know instinctively there's something she wants to say. I nod and wait as she fixes her gaze on my tiny wheelie case but seems to be staring straight through it.

'Look, I just want to check. I mean, that you're all right about all of this.' I put the laptop down and she sits down on the edge of the bed.

'All right about what, Mum?' I try to keep the irritation out of my voice. She's not going to get cold feet now, is she?

She shuffles backwards until she's sitting in the middle of the bed and her legs are off the ground. I wait for her to reply but she looks at her hands and says nothing.

'Look, Mum. If you mean am I still all right about meeting my dad after all these years, then yes, I'm still all right. I'm ready. The question is, are *you*?'

Mum sighs and looks up at me at last.

'I can't help wondering if we're doing the right thing. Going on a TV show, doing this so... publicly. It's a family matter. Isn't that something that should be private, just between us, our family?'

I literally can't believe what mum is saying. To come up with these arguments now! When everything's finally fallen into place? She senses my mood changing – she of all people knows when my anger threatens to get the better of me and boil over, from years of experience. I do my best not to lose my temper. *Breathe...*

I keep my voice steady and controlled. 'Mum. Listen. We're all packed, we've signed the forms, got the tickets, booked the hotel, the filming schedule's been confirmed – everything's in place. Are you actually saying you're thinking of changing your mind?'

Mum twirls a strand of her hair and then presses it between her lips. She won't look me in the eye. She stares up at the ceiling. And I wait for an answer. It's no good. However patient I try to be, I'm just not cut out for 'cool and calm under pressure'. It must be in my DNA.

'Mum – you can't! We've committed to it.' I know what Mum's like about sticking to things once you've made a commitment. She sits motionless like a statue. I try another angle.

'Charlie told everyone in our tutor group that

we're going to be on a TV show. I won't be able to show my face at school if it never happens.' As soon as the words are out of my mouth, I realise how hollow and meaningless they sound. Obviously, it doesn't matter what other people think. This is more important than scoring points with the popular girls. What's more, my voice is starting to sound whiney and desperate. I need to remind Mum about the real reason for the trip.

'Look, Mum. I can understand that this is going to be difficult for you. But you always taught me not to run away from situations that are difficult. I need to meet my dad. I need to know where he is, what he looks like, if he's got a hot temper just like me. I've always wanted to find out who my dad is. You said yourself: *it's something I should know.*'

'But I've agreed to help you find him. It's not that. Look, I think we've got enough of an idea of where to start looking for him ourselves. We could do this on our own. Leave all the TV stuff out of it. It's not a matter for public entertainment. This is about us. It's our lives we're talking about here. And what about Alexandros's life? What will all this attention do to his family? Can you imagine if he is married with children and he's going to have to come face to face with the daughter he never knew about? It could cause all sorts of trouble.'

'Well, I'm sorry about that but it's not my fault. I'm not some terrible secret to be kept hidden for the rest of my life. I didn't ask to be born!'

Mum is suddenly on her feet and I can see she's furious.

'Well, I didn't ask for it either, but you came along and here we are!' The words tumble out of her mouth at high speed, then a shocked silence surrounds us.

I don't think I've ever seen her angry before, not like this. She sometimes gets annoyed when things get broken or don't work properly, but she's usually pretty calm. She clamps her hand over her mouth but there's no point, the words have already escaped. They float in the air between us and echo in my ears. *I didn't ask for it either?*

I can still hear that sentence replaying in my head, over and over. In the nanoseconds after my brain processes what the words mean, my heart twists with a pang of pure despair and the anger seeps out of me like a slowly deflating balloon.

She didn't ask to have a daughter she had to bring up alone.

She didn't ask to have me.

She never wanted me.

Her eyes are wide and starey and she looks horrified. What does this mean? Has my whole life been a lie? I always thought Mum loved me, was proud of me. Is she saying she wishes I'd never been born?

'You know I didn't mean that, love,' she says, holding out her arms. I spring off the bed and refuse to speak or let her touch me.

'Get out of my room,' I order, my voice controlled but tinged with menace. Mum bites her lip and hangs her head. Then she does what she's told. I slam the door behind her.

All I can think is how I can't wait to meet my dad now. I need to find him more desperately than ever. He'll understand. I just know *he'll* be happy when he finds out about me. If Mum never really wanted me, at least I'm about to find the parent that does.

I'll show her. When she sees me with my dad she'll realise what she's done and she'll be sorry.

CHAPTER EIGHTEEN

'Wow, this is amazing,' gushes Charlie, shoving handfuls of the complimentary pretzels into her mouth and squeezing three bottles of Coke into her enormous handbag. 'I've never been in a VIP lounge before. I feel like a proper celeb!'

'Er, I don't think you're supposed to take those with you,' I tell her, shaking my head like I'm telling her off, though really I'm just as excited as she is. This is amazing. I mean I knew the TV company was going to take care of us, but Charlie's right, it's like we're royalty or something.

I curl up on one of the huge seats, sip my Coke and stare across the lounge at my auntie and Bernard, who are fussing over their bags. I've never seen so many suitcases and holdalls. It's mostly Bernard's stuff. I wonder how many outfits he's got and if he's going to have time to wear them all in a week. Gran's quizzing a uniformed waiter about the food and is having trouble believing that the gourmet sandwiches are free. 'Well, that's great. It's all free you say? Yes, but when you say "free" do you mean they are *really* free? Are you sure you're not going to charge us later on? I'd hate to come home to a big bill I hadn't been expecting.' Eventually, he manages to convince her and she piles up a tray with food, then comes over and sits down between us.

'Girls, get yourselves some of these sandwiches,' she urges, nodding over at the display on the counter. 'You can choose anything you want: salmon and rocket, avocado and bacon, beef and horseradish. Don't they sound fancy? None of your cheese and onion or mashed egg here. And the young man says it's all free. Can you believe it?'

Charlie agrees, nodding with the confidence of a lucky tourist who's quickly become accustomed to the finer things on offer. 'Free magazines, too, Gran. Look, this one's your favourite. It's even got some Sudoku puzzles at the back.'

I glance nervously at the glass doors. Half an hour to go until we take off and Mum's still nowhere to be seen. She'd said she wanted to have a 'chat' with Mark, the researcher, before we left the house, so I'd got in the taxi with Auntie Tash, Bernard, Charlie and Gran. Now I'm beginning to wonder what's holding her up. My insides turn cold at the thought that Mum might have changed her mind. She wouldn't do that to us now, surely?

Then the doors suddenly slide open and Mark strides in, Mum following behind. She doesn't look too happy but Mark is all smiles, hugging Gran, shaking hands with Bernard and making sure we're all comfortable. 'What do you think of the VIP lounge, Olivia?' he smiles in my direction, while Mum flops down next to me and stares into space. I shrug and Charlie butts in, showing Mark the drinks in her bag.

Mum stares ahead and gives the impression of someone who's about to be given a prison sentence, not whisked away to a beautiful country to meet the love of her life (her words, as I remember). I don't understand and I'm determined not to let her spoil this for me. I mean, what's the worst that can happen? Even if Alexandros is happily married to someone else, won't it still be better to know once and for all? It's been a mystery for too long. No, not a mystery: a secret. I've been a secret and I don't want to be one anymore.

Gran comes bustling over, flapping one of the magazines. 'Nine letters. A denial or dismissal. Second letter, "e".'

Mum ignores her, so I peer at the crossword and pretend to be helping Gran think of the word, when really all I can think of is that I'm about to get on a plane to fly to Greece to meet my father! I mean, how epic is that? I glance at Mum and her sullen face irritates me so much I have to take a deep breath and let it out slowly to the count of five, like it shows you on the anger management app.

'Rejection,' says Mum, still staring into space.

'Ah, yes, that's it,' nods Gran, carefully marking

the letters into the little white squares and mumbling to herself. She taps the pen on her front teeth as she works on the next clue.

I wish Mum wasn't being such a drama queen. I mean, can't she just shake herself out of this mood, even if it's just for my sake? I'm pretty sure that's what she would say if it was me sitting there with a face like thunder, or a face like a wet weekend in Wales, as she'd call it.

Mark's got a shiny orange suitcase with the *Find Your Family* (FYF) logo across the front, announcing to the world that he is in charge of our group and we are VIPs, on our way to make a TV show in a foreign country. He pulls out a clipboard from his shoulder bag and says he wants to run through a few things before we board. As he starts talking I have another one of those moments when what we're about to do hits me, and I'm almost breathless for a few seconds. It's really happening: this is it.

He beckons Auntie Tash and Bernard over so they can hear better. Gran ignores him and carries on with her crossword.

'So, guys, here we are. Now, before we leave, there are a few contractual obligations Ros has asked me to remind you of.' He glances at the sheet of paper. 'As you will remember from the contracts you all signed, there is to be no social media contact during the filming period. Are we all clear on that?'

A low mumble travels through the assembled

group, like an audible Mexican wave, only without the smiles or enthusiasm. 'So, that means, no Twitter, no Snapchat, no Insta, Facebook, WhatsApp, TikTok – nothing. Not until the filming is finished and Ros gives the all-clear. *All clear* about that? Yes? Sorry, just my little joke…'

Charlie blows a huge pink bubble until it pops and leave strands of gum dangling from her bottom lip. She's only taken up the habit because she knows it annoys Bernard. I know what's she's thinking – there's no way she's going to be able to resist updating her social media feeds. She blinks innocently at Rob. 'Can't we at least take pictures?' she asks. 'I mean, as long as we don't post them until after the filming.'

Mark nods. 'Of course you can. But, I must stress that failure to adhere to contractual obligations could result in your eviction from the show or, at the discretion of the management, the total cancellation of the show.' He's reading from the small print off the form as though he's recited these lines many times before. 'And, I ought to mention, any breach of the regulations as set down in the contracts will also be subject to a fine equal to the costs incurred by FYF Productions Limited during the research, preparation, planning and filming stages of the abovementioned episode.' Mum rolls her eyes and folds her arms as if it's the final straw. Charlie gulps and slips her phone into her back pocket. Just the mention of fines and the suggestion of lawyers chasing us for big sums of money is enough to remind us that we've signed up for something major, and if we want to get out of it, here is our chance. Everyone goes quiet and studies their shoes. The air suddenly seems a little chillier. Gran tries to double-wrap her cardigan around herself, murmuring about the air conditioning. I remind myself we are not prisoners, we are guests of a TV company about to be reunited with a long-lost family member. Anyway, I've never heard of a guest from a TV show being sued for breaking their contract. It's probably just a standard legal thing, a formality.

Charlie pulls a pink fluffy sweater from her TARDIS-like handbag and pulls it on over her head. She hates being cold. 'Brrrr. At least we're going somewhere hot,' she looks at her watch and does some mental maths. 'Just think, Ol. We'll be sunning ourselves in hot, sunny Greece in about … ohhh… four hours from now.'

Now we're boarding, and turning left at the top of the steps into the Club Class seats. And Charlie is squealing because we've only ever flown economy before and we thought *that* was great, but now we're being shown how the other half live and what we've been missing. She throws herself into one of the huge seats and reclines it so that her legs are stretched out in front of her. There's a goodie bag in the side pocket and she pulls out free headphones, an eye mask and a tiny bottle of posh moisturiser. I burrow into the seat next to her and we 'oooh' and 'ahhh' over the freebies and start studying the in-flight menu, even though we're still full from the snacks in the VIP lounge.

'Why aren't all rich people fat?' wonders Charlie, weighing up the choice of salted caramel milkshake and pretzels, or green tea or kiwi and kale juice with dried guava slices.

We're so engrossed I don't notice straight away that Mum's sat down in the seat next to mine. She's still got that far away, sad look and doesn't say a word.

'Mum – you okay?' I ask softly, touching her gently on the arm.

She smiles vaguely in my direction and pats my hand. 'Don't worry, love. It's all going to be fine,' she tells me, as if I'm the one who needs reassurance. Of course it's going to be fine, I want to say. I'm not worried about that. It's going to be amazing. I want to say those things. But I don't.

CHAPTER NINETEEN

'Your dad must be one of the most mysterious people on the planet,' decides Charlie, scrolling through images of people called Alexandros Papadopoulos on her phone. 'I mean, we even know his home village and he still doesn't show up on a Google search.' I frown and look over her shoulder, as picture after picture of dark-haired men, some serious, some in party-mode, all with an unmistakeable Mediterranean 'look', whizz past, making me feel dizzy. 'How do you know one of those pictures isn't him?' I ask, squeezing my eyes shut to give my retinas a break from trying to focus on so many headshots. Charlie ignores my question and expands on her theory. 'Maybe Greeks don't use Facebook. Or maybe he's living in some totally remote place with no wi-fi.'

'Too many maybes,' I say with a sigh, shaking my head in frustration. 'And would you mind stopping that now – it's not going to tell us anything. Besides, there's no need to keep searching now. The TV show's done all the hard work for us. We'll be meeting him in person soon and you can ask him all about his social media profile, or lack of it.'

Charlie doesn't seem to pick up on the irritation in my voice. She puts her phone down and looks me in the eye for once. 'Can you believe it, Ol? You're going to meet him. Finally. What do you think he'll be like?'

I've been wondering this, too. Obsessing, to be more accurate. I imagine him as tall, dark-haired and, well, handsome, obviously. What at cliché! Mum still swears she doesn't have any pictures of him even though I've been on and on at her. I asked if any of her uni friends would have one, but she said she'd lost touch with most of them and didn't want to make a big fuss about it after all this time. What she really meant was that she was too embarrassed to admit she had a daughter that was his that she'd kept quiet about all these years. That explained why she avoided reunions and tore up invitations to weddings, well most of them. There was that one she went to a few years ago, but she'd hardly talked about it after she'd come back. Always so mysterious! I wonder how she feels about her shameful secret (me) finally being revealed to the world! I look sideways to where she's sitting stiffly, mouth closed in a firm line, wearing her eye mask and with her earphones plugged in. No wonder she looks so moody. She's going to have some explaining to do. Well, isn't it about time? I can't feel sorry for her when I remind myself that she's the one who's caused all the problems, the years of dishonesty and secrecy. I don't even have an old, grainy Polaroid to go by so I'm left to my imagination. Sometimes I imagine him in a crisp white uniform, the captain of a ship in the Greek navy, travelling around the world on a peace-keeping mission. Other times, I picture him in a big, shiny office, wearing a smart grey suit, holding important meetings where million-euro deals are argued over and agreements eventually sealed with a confident handshake. The one fact I actually know about him is that he studied archaeology, though, and none of the scenarios for a life I've created for him in my mind seem to fit the identity of an archaeologist. Shouldn't he be digging up ancient burial sites somewhere, or teaching students or researching his own projects? I don't know why I can't imagine him doing that. Is it some sixth sense? Mind you, Mum has a first-class degree in archaeology and anthropology and she works in a college admissions office, so it's impossible to predict how adults might or might not use their qualifications. As far as I know, Mum had shown very little interest in ancient history, though she did once take me to the British Museum to see the relics from the Parthenon in Athens. I remember how smooth the statues were and wondering how the marble could have been chipped away so delicately to make the folds on a woman's robes and the details like the waves in her hair. But I'd been quite little then and had quickly got bored and pulled Mum away to the gift shop where I'd persuaded her to buy me a pencil sharpener shaped like a Greek vase.

I must have dropped off because now Charlie's shaking me and I'm opening my eyes and she's pointing out of the window and there's the bright blue sea glistening underneath us and in the distance I can see buildings and roads shining like ribbons and everything looks so bright and dazzling and there's a tear in my eye. I can't believe it. I'm about to arrive in Greece.

CHAPTER TWENTY

'Wow, check out that view!' Charlie pulls open the blinds and I shield my eyes as the sunlight floods the room, and my tired, sleepy brain tries to catch up. Ah yes, I remember now. I'm in Greece. We'd arrived yesterday in darkness and, tired out after the flight and the long coach ride, Charlie and I had decided to chill in our room and order room service, while the adults went out for dinner with Mark and Ros and some of the production crew.

The room we're sharing is, well, fabulous. I've never stayed in a five-star hotel before. We have a massive double bed each. The bathroom's all white marble with shiny gold fittings and is as big as our living room back at home.

With no warning, Charlie takes a run up and catapults herself onto my bed, bouncing me up off the mattress and into the air. 'Stop it, you idiot!' I shout, grabbing hold of the crisp sheets to stop myself falling off the bed. 'You're being evil. I'm not even awake yet.'

'Well, you'd better get up out of that bed pretty

quick, cos there's an empty pool out there, and if you can get ready in the next few minutes, we can have a swim before breakfast.'

I glance at my watch – ten to eight – and pick up the piece of paper on the bedside table. Breakfast is eight to eight-thirty. Mark had given us our schedules last night and the day was going to be tightly-packed with production meetings, briefing meetings, styling and rehearsals. I'd had no idea there was going to be so much to do. Silly me, I'd just imagined the part where I was introduced to my dad but, of course, there was much more to a TV show than the bit the audience got to see on the screen. I imagined all the different people involved, researchers, technicians, managers, important people with important jobs, all working so hard so that I could meet him at last. My insides fizzed uncomfortably and I couldn't tell if it was excitement or something else. Nerves, maybe? There seemed to be so much I hadn't prepared for. So much expected of me, but exactly what, I wasn't sure. I didn't want to look silly or let anyone down. What if it all went wrong and it was all my fault? What I needed was my mum giving me a hug and telling me it was all going to be okay, but there wasn't much chance of that. She was still upset. I could only hope that it would all be worthwhile and when she met Alexandros again, she'd be happy and she'd admit it had been a great idea after all.

It's just as well Charlie is there to drag me out of

bed, order me to put my swimsuit on, slide open the glass double doors that lead to the tile-covered terrace and pull me by the hand into the bright sunshine.

We race to the pool and dive-bomb into the deep end. The water is refreshing and cool, and we splash our way up and down, the exercise helping to distract me from my anxiety. Time is short though, and Charlie is determined not to miss breakfast, so we quickly dry off and get dressed and make our way down the hotel's long corridor to the restaurant, where Mum and Gran are already sitting at a table, tucking in to flaky pastries, Greek yoghurt and mini-bowls of sliced watermelon.

'Ah, there you are. We knocked on your door, but maybe you were in the shower or something,' explains Gran, drizzling a pool of golden honey into her yoghurt. 'Or maybe you had the hairdryer going, although, by the looks of things, neither of you have been near a hairdryer.' She nods towards Charlie's damp hair that lay loose on her shoulders. As quick as a flash, Charlie pulls a scrunchie off her wrist and sweeps up her hair into a sleek, chic doughnut nestling neatly on the top of her head. Amazing. How does she do it? I'd done my best to tuck my unruly curls behind my ears but I know they'll soon look like a straggly bush, if they don't already. I'm suddenly annoyed with myself for not waking up earlier; I could have used Charlie's straighteners, or at least tied my hair back before I went in the pool. I so want to look my best.

Everyone's going to be looking at me and I realise I'm not used to the discomfort of being the centre of attention.

. As if she's read my mind, Mum reaches into her handbag and passes me a pink hair elastic. 'Here, this should help for now,' she says softly.

Gran interrupts, 'Yes, that'll do it. Anyway, we'll be getting full hair and make-up tomorrow. Isn't that right, love?'

Charlie smirks. 'When you say "we", you mean Ol and Auntie Em, don't you, Gran? They're the stars of the show. The rest of us will just be in the audience, remember?'

'Well, we all want to look our best, you know,' Gran humphs, patting her grey curls protectively.

'Don't worry, Mum. I saw a hairdressers in the village we passed through on the way here. We can ask Mark about getting you an appointment. Ah, look, here's Mark now. Mark!'

Mark comes striding up to our table, looking red-faced and a bit sweaty already. 'Morning, everyone. Everything okay? It's sooo hot already. I've asked the manager if the aircon's working properly.' He pulls a cotton hanky out of his pocket and mops the back of his neck.

'Ah, Mark. A little heat is very welcome. You won't find me complaining,' Gran says.

'Gran feels the cold, don't you, Mum?' Mum smiles. 'Here, Mark, have some orange juice. It's freshly squeezed, and nice and cool.' She pours him a glass as he pulls up a chair and joins our table.

'Bit of a late night, was it?' she teases. Mark nods.

'Ended up getting whisked off to a club by some locals. Probably overdid it.'

'That explains why it's so quiet in here,' says Gran, looking round at the empty tables. 'Must be sleeping it off.'

'Yeah, the rest of the crew don't need to be around until later,' admits Mark, gulping down the juice in his glass like someone with severe dehydration. 'Maybe I should have thought that one through…'

Just then, there's a noise and we all turn to see what's going on by the entrance to the restaurant. It's Auntie Tash and Bernard and they seem to be having an argument with one of the uniformed hotel staff. Voices are being raised and we can hear Bernard's solid tones booming through the glass, 'What do you mean the restaurant is for guests only? I'm part of the TV show and I demand to be allowed to have a decent breakfast in a civilised environment. Let me through!' Mark jumps up and heads towards the commotion. He has a quiet word with the doorman who eventually shrugs and gives in.

'This is going to be fun,' whispers Charlie, helping herself to another bowl of fresh fruit.

'Absolutely outrageous,' huffs Bernard, landing heavily on a chair by our table. Mark's chair, to be exact. 'All I want is to sit down and have a nice breakfast without being molested by flea-bitten cats or eaten alive by mosquitoes,' he announces angrily.

Auntie Tash hovers uneasily and explains. 'It's the village accommodation. It's just not quite what Bernard's used to.'

'Sorry, I tried to get you guys a room here,' adds Mark. 'But they're fully booked. I thought the village house had a certain… rustic charm. Plus, there wasn't anything else available near here.'

'Rustic charm! Is that what you call it? Do you know the shower is just a hosepipe and a plughole and the toilet is… well, I won't go into that while you're eating your lovely, five-star breakfast.' Bernard eyes the pastries and fruit on the self-service counter. Mark passes him a plate. 'Here, you help yourselves. Don't worry, I'll sort it out with the manager.' Bernard does that thing with his neck that makes it go 'crack' but takes the plate and shuffles off towards the food display, Auntie Tash following obediently behind.

Charlie sniggers and Gran goes to tell her off but she's trying not to laugh too. Mark changes the subject. 'So, you'll need to be ready in…' He looks down at his watch. '…fifteen minutes. Busy day ahead.'

Mum and I had seen the schedule – we had to be filmed in a range of locations: eating ice creams on the beach, shopping for souvenirs in the village, sipping iced drinks outside a café, and do a series of mini-interviews where we talked about why we had contacted the show and what we were hoping to find out.

One of the things that surprised me most about the day, a day where just about everything was surprising, was the amount of 'rehearsing' we had to do. Charlie agreed with me when I pointed out that reality shows gave you the impression of being, well, 'real'. As in, not scripted, rehearsed, planned or prepared. But we had to practise everything. Where to stand, where to sit, what to do when Alexandros was brought onto the stage. Who would stand up first (Mum) and how to hug (by clasping each other's arms) and what to do next (kiss lightly on each cheek, left first, then right) before sitting down and waiting for the presenter, Lance, to ask us the pre-prepared questions (How does it feel to finally meet? What are you thinking? What do you want to ask first? Even that was scripted: Mum was supposed to smile and ask Alexandros if he thought she'd changed much, which I thought was a pretty ridiculous question and felt quite sorry for Mum having words put into her mouth). Ros kept telling us about this amazing picturesque location she'd found for the actual filming, but I was finding it hard to concentrate on what she was saying. Gran and Charlie sat in the empty studio, like a pretend audience and once or twice I caught Charlie's eye and could tell she was thinking the same as me. Being on a TV show might not be as much fun as we'd been expecting.

CHAPTER TWENTY-ONE

This is the day.

The day I meet my dad for the first time.

Finally.

I hardly slept last night. Excitement, fear, worry and joy jostled in my head and my heart, along with worry about doing something wrong and looking silly in front of all those people. At least Maya the make-up magician has managed to make me look presentable; I asked her to put on extra concealer to hide the dark circles under my eyes.

The stage is set. We take our places in a tiny, crumbling amphitheatre, perched on the edge of a cliff, against a backdrop of a baby blue sky melting into a turquoise sea. It really is spectacular, but I'm too nervous to take it in.

The floor manager counts down from ten and Lance turns to face the camera.

'Hello, and welcome to this very special episode of *Find Your Family*, all the way from sunny Greece!' he announces, his voice rising with excitement, the floor manager flapping his arms at the audience so they know when to start to whoop and clap. Apart from Gran, Auntie Tash, Bernard and Charlie, the audience is mostly made up of people who work on the show, plus a few of their friends and family who've come along for the ride. It's not a big audience, so they've been told to make a lot of noise to make it seem like a bigger crowd. Gran managed to get her hair done and the curls are sitting high and stiff on her head like a grey helmet. Auntie Tash looks a bit sunburned and Bernard keeps scratching at the mosquito bites on his face, but they do as they're told and keep clapping enthusiastically until they get the signal to stop. Charlie's eyes are like saucers and she keeps her gaze on the cameras, keeping ready, just in case they're turned on her.

And this is it. The moment is here. Lance introduces Alexandros and I see him for the first time as he come out from behind a screen and strides onto the stage, adjusting his baseball cap and straightening his aviators. The first thing I think is he's so short: why do I think that? Maybe because he looks as if he's borrowed his clothes from someone bigger. His trousers are too long and pool in baggy wrinkles at his ankles and his jacket's too long, too, the sleeves hanging down over his thick knuckles. I try to push the thought away, but even as I'm doing everything just as we rehearsed and hug him by the arms and kiss him lightly on both cheeks, and we sit down and Mum asks if she's changed much, and all I can think is why

don't I feel anything? I look at this man and feel...
nothing but a numb emptiness. How can this be?
He's my dad! I imagine handing over the shoebox
of letters to him, but I already know it's never going
to happen. Lance asks Mum if Alexandros has
changed much, and she nods, smiles and answers
with a vague little 'yes' and says how different he
looks with a beard. And I'm so confused all I want
to do is go home and cry, but I have to sit through
this horrible show and act like I'm really happy,
while Alexandros talks about how he's thought
about Mum over the years, and they have so much
catching up to do, but I notice he's not looking at
Mum or me while he's saying these things, but at
the audience, and I think about poor Mum and
wonder what she's feeling.

Then it's over. They're taking off our
microphones and Alexandros is shaking hands
with everyone, but I can't bear to go near him and
I just don't know why.

Charlie runs up and hugs me and tells me what
a great job I did and asks me how I feel but I can't
speak. Then Alexandros turns to Mum and says
we're invited to the village tonight to have a meal
with his family and meet all the relatives and how
they can't wait to meet us. Mum nods and smiles
and tries to look happy, but I know something's
wrong. Alexandros leans forward to kiss her but
she takes a step back. The weird thing is no one
seems to notice that Mum and I are uncomfortable.

Everyone's happy because the show went so well. Mark and Ros come over and say 'Great job' and 'You nailed it', and that the fees for our participation will be released in forty-eight hours, and here's the number of a counsellor if you need help to 'process your feelings', and they shake our hands, and everyone starts to pack up, and the studio begins to empty out.

Mum tries to pull Ros aside, but she shakes her head and says they can catch up later after she's finished the voiceovers. Mum gives up and takes me away from the chaos. We find a bench under the shade of a huddle of lemon trees.

'You okay?' she asks me, her voice shaking and her lower lip trembling slightly. I nod and attempt a smile but I can't do it and burst into tears instead. She passes me a tissue from her shoulder bag and I blow my nose noisily. 'Sorry, Mum. I don't know why I'm upset. I suppose I just expected… I don't know, I thought I would feel….' my voice trembles and I don't trust it to finish the sentence and instead blink away fresh tears.

Mum puts her arm around me and side-hugs me. 'I know. It's weird,' she agrees, with a deep sigh. 'He's like a stranger. I know we've both changed, but I never thought someone could change so much in what, fourteen years?'

I nod, but it's hard to believe. I try to imagine all the events that have taken place over the years and how much people can change over time. Mum carries on, 'I mean he looks *similar*, but...'

'I don't know why, but I imagined he'd be taller,' I say with a sniff.

'So did I!' smiles Mum. 'That's memories for you. Totally unreliable.' She goes quiet and seems to be considering saying something else, but changes her mind. 'Look, we'll go to this meal tonight, meet all your "long lost" relatives. It might help us to make sense of all this. It might help us to…'

I know what she's going to say and chime in and we chorus, 'Process our feelings!' We manage a weak laugh and for the first time in ages I feel like Mum and I are on the same page again.

'Sorry it wasn't what you expected,' Mum says quietly, and I know she feels bad because I'm upset, that's how it's always been, just me and Mum. But I feel bad, too, for putting her through this. She never asked for it.

'Sorry,' I whisper, tears welling up again.

'Sorry? You have nothing to be sorry about, my darling. *Nothing*. If anyone should be sorry, it's me. I should have been honest with you from the start. I don't know why I thought it would be a good idea to keep secrets from my own daughter.'

But *I* do. She was trying to protect me. To save me from disappointment. I've brought all this upon myself, and her. I'm going to cry again but then I don't, because Charlie bursts into our quiet space, breaking the spell and reminding us that there is a car waiting to take us back to the hotel and we need to get ready for the big family reunion tonight, which she clearly means to invite herself to.

CHAPTER TWENTY-TWO

Auntie Tash and Bernard are talking loudly and no one can get a word in, which suits me fine, because I really don't want anyone quizzing me on how it feels to finally meet my dad or whether he's what I expected or what the rest of the family is going to think of having a new member. We're all squashed into the taxi, Mum, Gran, Charlie, my auntie and Bernard, Mark and me. It's a seven-seater, but with so many big personalities to fit in, it feels cramped. Mark's full of energy, proud of how the filming went, telling us that the crew are leaving today and there'll be spare rooms going if Tash and Bernard want to relocate from the village.

Bernard is ecstatic. 'Oh, thank the Lord!' he announces, flinging his arms wide theatrically, nearly hitting Charlie in the face. 'Oi, careful,' she warns, pushing his freckly forearm away. He carries on, oblivious. 'At last, a proper hotel with proper facilities. Do you know that dump we were staying in doesn't even have a mini-bar?'

'To be fair, they've done their best to look after us,' my auntie points out. 'Maria, the owner, is very kind and her breakfasts are to die for: home-made pastries, freshly-squeezed orange juice from her own orange groves, and that goat's cheese she makes herself…'

'To die *from*, more like. That stuff's lethal!' Bernard disagrees at full volume. 'It *stinks* and it's probably not even pasteurised. It's a miracle we haven't had food poisoning.' His face reddens with outrage at the thought of this and my auntie shrugs and keeps quiet.

It's clear Bernard's made up his mind; he can't bear the thought of another second in a room with no mini-bar, so it's been agreed that we stop off at the village to pick up their belongings so they can move out straight away and come back with us to check in at the hotel. As the driver turns off the main road and onto a dusty track, we catch sight of the place Bernard can't wait to vacate. It's a pretty white-washed cottage with blue painted shutters and window-frames and rows of brightly-coloured flowers sprouting from buckets and terracotta pots, which line the pathway to the open front door. A large black cat yawns and looks up at us from under an olive tree and a couple of chickens wander around, pecking at tufts of grass. As the car comes to a stop, Bernard jumps out, not wasting any time in checking out and we follow, eager to stretch our legs and curious to see what all the fuss was about. A lace curtain covering the doorway is pulled aside, and a dark-haired lady steps out, smiling her welcome and putting out her hand, but before any introductions can be made, someone else steps out of the house behind her and we're all stunned into silence. It's Uncle Joe!

'Dad!' Charlie shrieks, before flinging herself at him. He hugs her and waves at the rest of us. 'Hi, everyone. How's it going? What have I missed?'

Soon, we're piling in to Maria's cool and inviting kitchen, where she pours glasses of home-made iced lemonade while my uncle tells us about his long, eventful journey by train, boat and bicycle.

'You could have just got the plane, it only takes a few hours,' Gran points out. 'You're not Phileas Fogg, you know!'

'Filly who?' says Charlie with a frown, wrinkling her nose.

Uncle Joe laughs good-naturedly. 'You know how I feel about air travel. Besides, I got to see most of Europe on my road trip. What an adventure! Then I heard about this beautiful spot and Maria's interest in eco-tourism. Lots to tell, but there's time for that later. The important thing now is, I wanted to be here for the big moment.' Turning to me, he adds, 'But Maria told me the filming was today. I'm sorry I missed the "big reveal", Ollie. I know you've wanted to meet your dad for a long time.'

'Forever,' I correct him happily, just glad to have my uncle here. But the reminder of the show brings the memories crowding back in. He must have seen from my face something was wrong, but he's too sensible, and sensitive, to mention it in front of everyone. Mum fills him in, telling him about the meal we're invited to tonight, and the invitation to meet the rest of the family.

'You'll come, won't you?' she urges. 'The whole family's invited.'

'Wouldn't miss it for the world,' Uncle Joe smiles. Charlie hugs him and for once doesn't seem to mind that he's unshaven and unwashed and dressed like someone who's been wearing the same clothes for a week. Which, come to think of it, he probably has.

'You can try out the new outdoor shower,' laughs Maria. 'We've just finished it. It works by filtering the grey water…'

Uncle Joe nods encouragingly as she starts to explain the workings of the new, environmentally-friendly plumbing system, Bernard emerges, suitcases in each fist and more bags tucked under his armpits. He stops in his tracks at the mention of where the waste water goes, rolls his eyes, and practically runs to the waiting taxi.

We say our goodbyes and arrange to pick up Uncle Joe later, but he insists he's going to find his way to Alexandros's place on his trusty bike. '*Rusty*, more like,' says Auntie Tash, curling her lip a little, but more as a joke than a criticism. We all stare at the ancient two-wheeler, and to be fair she's not wrong. Still, as Uncle Joe points out, it got him here and we all have to agree on that, at least. Bernard leans over the driver and honks the horn impatiently, so we all pile back into the taxi and head back to the hotel to get ready. It's going to be a long day. And night.

CHAPTER TWENTY-THREE

I'm glad I didn't wear the shimmery, blue dress for the show, because it means I can wear it for the evening where I get to meet my Greek family.

Something had stopped me and I don't know what. Maybe it was the dress of a confident person and I just hadn't been feeling that confident this morning. Whatever the reason, I feel ready to wear it now. Maybe it was the thought of having Uncle Joe there. I sit in front of the mirror and try not to worry about what everyone will think of me.

'I can't believe your dad came,' I say to Charlie, who's standing behind me, French-plaiting my hair, still damp from the shower. 'How come he didn't tell anyone?'

'You know he doesn't have a mobile phone anymore?' She sighs dramatically, as if she disapproves, but I sense she's actually quite proud of him. I mean, lots of people talk about saving the planet and being environmentally responsible, but how many people are prepared to actually put that into practice? 'You've got to admire his commitment, though,' I point out. 'And he went to all that trouble to get here.' I'm about to say something about him being my hero but that's way too cheesy. Instead, I ask Charlie what she thinks the evening to come will be like. She does her thinking face but quickly relaxes her facial muscles as she catches sight of herself in the mirror and leans towards her reflection, checking for frown lines on her forehead.

'I mean, it's going to be interesting, that's for sure,' she says, gripping handfuls of my hair firmly and expertly. 'Alexandros mentioned a big family. So expect lots of aunties and uncles and cousins you never knew you had. Oh, and he said you'll meet your grandma, too.'

My stomach flips over at the thought of all those people waiting to meet me. What will they think of me? Maybe my new grandma will disapprove of children being born outside of marriage, just like Gran does.

'Do you think Alexandros is married?' I realise as soon as I say this that it's been in the back of my mind since the show ended. He'd made no mention of a wife or children and neither had Lance, Mark, Ros, or any of the researchers.

'I didn't see a ring on his finger,' Charlie answers. 'But that doesn't necessarily mean anything. Lots of men don't wear wedding rings.'

I let out a long breath to calm myself, but the words spill out of me faster than I can control. 'Isn't it going to be weird if he's got a wife and mum gets introduced as the mother of his child and I find out I've got half-brothers or sisters?'

'Don't worry,' commands my cousin, tying up the end of my plait with a sparkly silver ribbon. 'It's not your problem. Let them worry about that. You concentrate on having fun and enjoying the moment. This is your moment, remember. You've talked about this for years...'

'Yes, but talking about it and imagining it is so different from actually being in the moment,' I point out, remembering the sinking feeling of disappointment in the TV studio. 'Maybe reality never lives up to your dreams.'

Charlie spins me round so I'm facing her. 'Look, what's the worst that can happen? If you don't like them, you never have to see them again. But at least you'll know. The mystery will be solved and it will be an end to all the secrecy. Besides,' she adds, reaching for her make-up bag. 'You never know. There might be some cute boys there.'

'Yueww,' I reply, wrinkling my nose.

'Stop!' orders my cousin. 'You, young lady, need to open your mind. Be ready for new experiences. We're teenagers, not kids.'

I don't reply. I suspect my cousin has a point. Even if it does sound like she gets these ideas off one of those 'self-help' podcasts she listens to.

Mark knocks at the door and strides in. 'Taxi's here! Or rather *taxis*,' he announces, doing a comic twirl to show off his white linen suit. 'Shows off the tan to its best, don't you think?'

'Oh, hi, Mark. Do come in, won't you?' Charlie deadpans.

Ignoring her, he slides his sunglasses to the top of his head and walks over to the mirror, leans over my shoulder and peers at my reflection, as Charlie dabs my eyelids with some glittery turquoise eye shadow.

'Hey, girl, you looking goooood!' he nods.

'Yeah, it's actually not all about you, you know, Mark? This is a big night for Ol. For our whole family actually.'

'Okay, okay, I know, I'm just a bit excited, that's all,' he nods, doing a little pout like he can't stand anyone being a bit upset. 'You're looking fabulous, too, as ever,' he soothes, knowing just how to get on Charlie's good side. 'Hey, I know, we need some music.' He fiddles with Charlie's phone and turns the volume up full.

'Catwalk time!'

Mark struts down the middle of the room, eyes focused on a pretend audience of fans, puts his hand on his hip, does a spot turn, puts his hand on his other hip and sashays back down the carpet.

'Your turn,' he insists, pulling Charlie away from me and getting her into position. She can't help laughing and joins in the 'show', doing an exaggerated hip-swivelling swagger down the room and back, in time to the music. Now it's my turn. I hate doing things like this and I know I'm going to look like an idiot, not all cool and elegant like my cousin, but then I look at Mark and he's laughing and carefree and clapping along to the beat and next thing I know Charlie's pushing me gently towards the 'catwalk' and I find myself doing the model-walk-thing and I catch sight of myself in the mirror and I'm laughing too and the silky blue dress is sweeping from side to side, slowly and smoothly, like waves running up and down a beach. This is fun!

The song ends and we have a quick group hug, before Charlie grabs her phone, switches it off and slips it into her back pocket. 'Come on,' she says. 'Let's meet the Greeks!'

CHAPTER TWENTY-FOUR

As the taxi speeds along the mountain roads that skim the edge of the cliffside, we watch the huge orange sun lower itself slowly towards the horizon. It gets darker quite suddenly: first, a soft evening light spreads over the pretty houses we pass, soon giving way to an inky darkness. The driver slows down and peers into the gloom, trying to locate the village taverna, before pulling up beside a gateway to a hidden courtyard.

We step through the opening and Charlie gasps. 'Awww – pretty!' The taverna tables are covered with blue and white check cloths and lit by an overhead canopy of twinkly fairy lights strung between the trees. Ros is sitting at the head of the table, a cigarette in one hand and a glass of beer in the other. Mum, Auntie Tash, Bernard and Gran are already here, and Ros looks on silently, dragging long and hard on her cigarette, while they huddle around Alexandros and a group of guys of a similar age, making introductions, shaking hands. They catch sight of us and Alexandros waves us over.

'Come and meet your family!' he smiles at me, nodding enthusiastically in our direction. 'This is my cousin, Alexandros, we call him Alex,' he says, clapping his hand heavily on his cousin's shoulder. Alex nods shyly; he's quite a bit younger than 'dad' Alex and looks unused to formal introductions. Then again, formal introductions to family members you never knew you had who pop up from nowhere probably isn't something anyone can get used to. There are two more Alexes, introduced as 'Big Alex' and 'Small Alex', all slight variations on stocky and dark-haired with dark green eyes, more like brothers. 'What do you mean? Did they run out of names or something?' asks Gran in confusion. 'Why on earth are you all called "Alex"?'

'It's a family tradition,' explains Alexandros. We name the first son in every family after his grandfather, his father's father. We are all named after the same Grandfather Alexandros.' Gran looks like she's got more to say on the subject, but Alexandros opens his hands in a welcoming gesture and announces to the assembled group:

'And this beautiful young lady, is my daughter, Olivia.'

There's a hush and I walk forward. He takes my hands in his and looks me over with pride. 'Beautiful girl,' he nods, looking around at his cousins to make sure they agree. 'Do you think she looks like her dad?'

An awkward moment follows, when no one

speaks. Mum and Ros lock eyes for a second before Ros shifts her gaze and takes a long gulp from her beer glass. Bernard doesn't seem to notice, and asks if anyone would like a drink and the chatter starts up again, with Alexandros shaking his head and telling Bernard not to worry, everything is taken care of, the drinks and food are on their way. 'We even have champagne,' he smiles, 'but maybe you would like to start with a nice cold beer.' He shouts over to the waiter hovering in the doorway, and tells us to take our seats. He pulls out a chair for Mum and she sits down obediently. We fill the spaces around the table but somehow I had thought there'd be more people. Aunties, uncles, cousins, maybe grandparents. I look around and do a quick count. Just five more people than the group I came with. Is this it? A few guys all called Alex? Is this my Greek family?

Charlie sits next to me and pulls her chair close.

'This place is so cute,' she smiles. 'Do you think more people are coming?' We look around and the empty tables and I shrug. She leans over to Alexandros and asks him, 'Hey, Alex. Are you expecting more people tonight?' Alexandros's face clouds for a nano-second, then fixes itself into an unconvincing smile. 'Yes, of course. Don't worry, Greeks are always late.' All the Alexes nod in agreement.

'Can we order food now, though?' Mark pipes up, his beetroot face a picture of worry. 'I'm starving.'

'Of course, don't worry. It is all taken care of.'

'Er, so where's the menu?' Mark asks, looking around hopefully.

Alexandros waves his hand dismissively and his bottom lip juts out in a little pout as he elaborates. 'No menu. This is Greece. We have whatever is fresh from the kitchen today. Maybe fish, maybe a little *pasticcio*, *salata* – salad…'

'Chips?' Mark prompts, his eyes big at the thought of the dishes to come. Is the guy *ever* not hungry?

Alexandros smiles and nods as if he's reassuring a child. 'Yeeeesss, of course, chips. Anything you want.'

Mark smiles back, clearly relieved his isn't going to have to sit in the restaurant getting hungrier and hungrier waiting for some more people to turn up. Alexandros gives him a little wink and Mark blushes so that his cheeks become a tiny bit redder. Gran tears off a bit of bread that's been placed in chunks in baskets around the table and nods approvingly. 'I need to get the recipe,' she says, turning to Small Alex. 'There's really nothing better than this Greek bread. I've never tasted the like.'

'And she should know,' Auntie Tash jumps in. 'Mum's famous for her baking.'

'Ah, I hope we can come and visit you in England one day and try your lovely food,' Small Alex says politely. I search Gran's face for her reaction to this. How does she feel about having a whole Greek family she never even knew about a few months ago descend on her home expecting to sample her cooking? Gran smiles happily, apparently fine with this idea. So far so good.

Drinks start to arrive, lots of ice and jugs of water, beers, wine, bottles of Coke. Then Uncle Joe appears in the entrance, climbing off his bike and stowing it under one of the trees. He runs his fingers through his hair and smiles, kisses Charlie, then me, and sits down in the empty chair next to Mum. She looks relieved. I think she was worried Alexandros was going to claim that seat. It doesn't seem right to put my mum and dad together, as a couple. While I try to work out why that is, the waiter hands Uncle Joe a beer and he takes a long, grateful glug. His 'English scruff' look translates well: here, he comes across more as 'intrepid explorer', complete with neatly trimmed beard, sun-bleached hair, golden tan, all lean and toned from the cycling. He's a bit sweaty from the bike ride but he's wearing a white linen shirt that shows off his tan and for once Charlie seems to approve. 'Been shopping, Dad?' she says with an approvingly smile. 'Suits you.' Even Auntie Tash does a double take, sipping from her glass thoughtfully, while Bernard slaps mosquito repellent all over his face and mutters something about launching an attack and his plans to annihilate the unsuspecting blood-sucking enemy.

'I had to look my best for this auspicious occasion.' He smiles towards me and does a little bow.

'So, how are feeling, Ollie? Must be a lot to take in,' my auntie wonders out loud.

It's the first time anyone's asked me since I met Alexandros and I search my brain for the right answer, while all eyes are suddenly on me.

I look over at the man I only met for the first time earlier today, the man I've dreamed about meeting for as long as I can remember. What can I say? I can't spoil this moment and tell everyone I feel nothing like I expected to.

I force my face to smile and nod frantically, while I think of something to fill the silence.

Uncle Joe rescues me, saying, 'I'm sure Olivia is too excited to put it into words. Give her some time,' nodding at the waiter and pointing to his empty beer bottle. A murmur of agreement follows and the chatter starts up again. I mouth a silent 'thanks' in his direction and then Charlie's asking me if I want to try the starters and passes me a plate of something pink and white. I spear a small piece onto the end of my fork and bite into it. It's chewy but doesn't taste of much. 'What is it?' I ask her.

She takes a bit and chews it warily.

'Is octopus,' explains Small Alex. Caught this morning and grilled tonight. Fresh-fresh,' he adds proudly.

Charlie's eyes widen and she freezes. I really

hope she's not going to spit it out. That would look so rude. 'You like?' Small Alex asks and she nods. We watch while she forces herself to swallow it, helping it down with a mouthful of Coke. Uncle Joe is trying not to laugh and Small Alex offers him the plate. He shakes his head, 'I'm vegan,' he answers politely. 'I don't eat animal products.'

Small Alex looks confused for a second but puts the plate down and picks up another. 'You like *dolmades* – vine leaves? They are stuffed with rice. No meat products.'

Uncle Joe takes one and puts it on his plate.

Small Alex nods approvingly. 'Has only some lamb. Tiny bit. Is nothing.'

Uncle Joe piles his plate with salad and slides the vine leaf onto my plate when no one's looking.

As it turns out, there are plenty of dishes to choose from and something for everyone: giant white beans in sticky tomato sauce, fried courgette flowers (who knew courgettes had a flower?), spinach and cheese pastries, chicken kebabs, lamb kebabs, cheese-filled burgers, grilled tiny fish and swordfish steaks.

There's soon a noisy mixture of voices and then someone puts on some Greek music in the background.

Alexandros is merry and is talking loudly, telling his cousins and my mum some hilarious story by the sound of it. I can't hear what he's saying but he's clearly got to the punchlines and roars with laughter, throwing his head back, thoroughly pleased with himself. I have a horrible feeling about him – I feel sure he's hiding something. Seeing him and Mum together really confuses me. He was supposed to be the love of her life, so why does she act so unfriendly around him and look at him so coldly? What hasn't she told me? There must be more to the story. There's something about him that makes me uneasy, and I've only just met him. What on earth is going on? Why do I feel like that about my own dad? I'm furious with myself, with him, with mum, with everyone. He puts his arm on my mum's shoulder and she shrugs it off lightly. Maybe he's just a bit annoying when he gets drunk. Some people are. I remind myself that I haven't given him a chance yet. We hardly know each other. I have to give it time. Maybe Mum will explain more and it will all start to make more sense.

Big Alex is telling a story about the scrapes he would get into with his cousins, when they were boys. 'One day, Alexandros saw some tourists go swimming after dark. They were, how do you say *horis ruha*?' he asks, turning to Small Alex. 'Without clothes,' nods his cousin helpfully. 'Yes, these guys, they decided to leave their clothes on the sand and go in the sea for swimming, and Alexandros, he waits until they are far out in the sea, and he takes their clothes.' All the Alexes hoot with laughter at the memory. Even Gran can't help a tiny smile.

Alexandros wipes tears of laughter from his eyes. 'They were...' He giggles. 'They were running up and down the beach, shouting, looking everywhere.'

'Yes,' joins in Big Alex, 'in the end they found them, on a chair, right in front of the busiest beach bar in the village!' 'They had to grab their clothes and run. I have never seen two guys run away so fast!' Alexandros slaps his thigh and guffaws. 'And another time, when my cousin was a teenager,' continues Big Alex, clearly getting into his stride as he launches into another tale of Alexandros's fondness for pranks, 'he was on a school trip to Italy with the Scouts. The last night, he and his friends decided to take all of the sleeping bags out of the tents and...'

'That's strange.' It's Mum's voice, coming from nowhere, cutting off the flow of cheerful banter. 'You told me you'd never been out of Greece until you went to university in England.' The smile slides from Alex's face. 'Or have I got that wrong?'

A hollow silence fills the space the laughter had occupied moments ago. The Alexes look at each other and it feels like everyone's holding their breath, waiting for someone to break the awkward spell. Alexandros looks over at Mum and shrugs. 'You have a very good memory, my dear,' he says, narrowing his eyes and pointing his forefinger in her direction. 'But I think you are mistaken. I said I had never *lived* outside of Greece before I went to university.' Alexandros smiles as if to congratulate himself for clearing up the misunderstanding. Big Alex's shoulders relax and the tense atmosphere eases. Mum opens her mouth as if to say something but changes her mind and turns to Uncle Joe instead.

The carefree laughter is replaced with hushed whispers; the group is now broken up into pairs and smaller groups. There's a dull ache in the bottom of my stomach and when Uncle Joe passes me a dish of pastries, I realise I've lost my appetite. I wish I knew why I just can't shake this feeling that Alexandros is hiding something. I look over at Mum and wonder what is going through her head. Suddenly I feel tired and just want the evening to be over. Why is it that the thought of going home and getting back into my own bed, back to my old life, just me and Mum, suddenly seems so attractive? I think of all the years I spent looking forward to this day, yearning and praying for it to come. Now the day has come and all I can think of is how soon we can get away. *What is wrong with me?*

More dishes emerge from the kitchen, the waiter refilling glasses, taking away empty platters and replacing ice-filled water jugs. Charlie starts a game of 'Never Have I Ever' with the Alexes.

'Never have I ever… cheated on a test at school,' Charlie says, avoiding her mum's look of disapproval. The Alexes roar with laughter.

'For me, I can say, 'Never have I ever NOT cheated on a test at school,' roars Alexandros, clinking glasses with Mark and emptying his glass with three noisy gulps. He says something about celebrating his inheritance from his grandfather, bangs the glass down heavily, and looks around for the waiter.

'This guy really is hilarious,' Gran whispers, pulling up a chair next to me and sliding in to it. I'm so surprised at how fast Gran has warmed to him, the mysterious stranger until now only a mythical figure she associated with bringing shame onto the family name, it takes a minute to process what I already know. My life will never go back to the way it was. When I go home, I will be different. Our family has changed, now I have unravelled the mystery of my missing dad. Gran has clearly found a fond place in her heart for Alexandros. I wish I could feel the same. I think about the box of cards and letters back in the hotel room, and wonder if I'll ever hand them over. Even as I try to picture the scene in my head, I can't imagine it's ever going to happen. At least, not until I've got to know the guy. He is, and remains, a stranger I happen to be related to. I glance over at Mum. I need to ask her … I don't know what, exactly, but I need to find out more about their past. I want to know how they first met and what brought them together; maybe if I got them to tell me some stories about their student days and started to fill in the gaps, it would all seem more … real, somehow. It might be easier for me to accept this new man in our lives is really my father. But Mum's seat is empty. So is Uncle Joe's. Where could they have got to?

Alexandros, his cousins and Mark are getting louder and drunker. Alexandros makes a toast to his inheritance, explaining how his grandfather left a piece of land and an olive grove to the first of his grandchildren to have a child, which seems to be a great cause for celebration. Only Small Alex gives any impression of remembering that we are guests, family members, here to meet our relatives, not clueless tourists just here for the sun, sea and booze.

Gales of hysterical laughter can be heard from the other Alexes, clustered around Mark's end of the table. Ros, who has been quiet all evening, stubs out her cigarette and starts to say her goodbyes. She comes over to give us a hug and says she'll call Mum later, to say goodbye, before her early flight. Ros places her hands on my shoulders and looks into my eyes. 'You've been amazing, Olivia, really amazing. Don't forget, you can always get in touch with me if you need anything. Ever.' She holds my gaze as if she's trying to convey some deeply meaningful message but I'm not sure what exactly. I mean, Ros has hardly paid me any attention up until now; she always left that to Mark. And now that the filming is all done and the editing has begun, I don't expect to ever hear from her again.

Charlie flings her arms around Ros and kisses the air around her cheeks. For a second, I start to wonder why Charlie is suddenly being so friendly to Ros. Then, she steps back, takes a dramatic breath and says, 'It's been an amazing experience. I'm so proud to have been part of it,' she smiles coyly, adding, 'Maybe you'll win that TV Gold award and invite us to the ceremony.' Ah, now it makes sense.

Ros gathers her cashmere around her shoulders against a light breeze coming off the sea. 'Let's wait and see what happens,' she answers vaguely, taking one long, last look around the group seated at the table. Gran gives her a little wave, Auntie Tash flutters her fingertips and Bernard, his arm draped around my aunt's suntanned shoulder, tips his wineglass and nods in Ros's direction, before going back to gazing lovingly at his prize. Charlie nudges me and whispers 'Ugggh! *Gross!*' I know I need to distract her before she shouts at them to 'Get a room!' I turn to Small Alex and ask if he still thinks some more family members are going to show up. He shrugs and takes some tiny sips of his coke. 'Probably, but perhaps much later.' He leans forward so he can be heard against the music and loud voices, and adds, 'I know *Yiayia* will be so happy to meet you. And your mother. And your mother's mother!'

'*Yiayia*?' I repeat.

'Sorry, is Greek word for "grandmother", he

explains. 'Maybe tomorrow, you can go to see her. She lives in the next village.'

I hadn't thought about the chances of having a Greek granny.

I tried to picture her. Would she be like the old ladies dressed head-to-toe in black that we'd seen in the village, sitting outside their houses, gossiping in pairs about passers-by, or hefting bags of shopping up the steep cobbled streets under the hot morning sun?

'Does she know about me, and the TV show, and everything?' I ask shyly. I still don't know if Alexandros and his family think of me as a guilty secret or a welcome surprise.

Alex waggles his head from side to side before he answers. 'Of course,' he replies at last, his voice light and carefree but his eyes determined to avoid mine. 'Look,' he adds, 'Greeks, they love children. Just wait. She will be, how do you say, over the moon.'

Alex seems keen to change the subject and waves at Mum and Uncle Joe as they emerge from the doorway to the taverna's kitchen. Mum frowns and Uncle Joe raises a hand in Alex's direction.

'Ros just left,' I explain to Mum. 'She said she'll call you later, before her flight.'

Mum nods but her face remains frozen.

She looks over at Alexandros, now standing in the middle of the group, dancing about, a bottle of beer in each hand, clearly having a great night. She turns to me.

'I think it's probably best if you two go back to the hotel, too. It's getting late.'

Uncle Joe shrugs apologetically, 'I'd give you a lift, but you wouldn't both fit on the crossbar,' he says. I don't know what he and Mum have been talking about but the mood has definitely shifted and the air feels a little more chilly. Bernard and Auntie Tash get up and come over. The drunken Alexes and Mark are singing along to a song Alexandros is playing on his phone and Bernard has to shout to be heard.

'Natasha and I are ready to go home,' he bawls in Mum's ear. 'Can we give you a lift back to the hotel?'

Mum shakes her head. 'I think I'll stay for a bit, thanks. But could you take these two with you?' She places a hand on my shoulder and fiddles with the blue ribbon strap of my dress. 'It's been a long day.' Mum cups my cheek with her palm and looks like she might cry. That would be too embarrassing for words. I hate it when she gets teary and sentimental. I nod vigorously, eager to leave before she says something to make us all cringe. We say our goodbyes and Small Alex tries to say something about meeting *Yiayia* in the village tomorrow and Alexandros and his cousins nod energetically and agree what a great idea it is, but I can tell they're so drunk they might not even remember having this conversation and will probably be sleeping off hangovers tomorrow. Plus, they don't show any signs of slowing down or calling it a night.

As we clamber into Bernard's hire car, Mark's voice can be heard over the loud music, shouting 'Let's party! The night is young!' A plate smashes noisily on the stones of the courtyard and a cheer of 'Opah!' goes up.

It's not until we are pulling up at the car park of the hotel that Auntie Tash turns to me and Charlie on the the back seat. 'Oh my lord!' she gasps, clamping her palm to her forehead. 'We forgot Gran!'

CHAPTER TWENTY-FIVE

'Can't believe how totally annoying those people are,' sighs Charlie, furiously kicking off her sandals. I throw myself backwards on to the bed and stare up at the ceiling. She means her mum and Bernard, of course, who sent us off to bed while they sped back to the village. What happened there? I try to picture when I last saw my gran. How on earth could we have left the taverna without her noticing?

'Well, what did you expect them to do? Leave Gran to find her own way home?' I ask her irritably.

Charlie's head whips round and she gives a low whistle. 'Ooooohkay, what's up, Ol? Come on, out with it!' she demands. I sit up quickly but instead of answering, I start undoing my French braids with a growing fury that has been burning slowly all day but has now, I realise, reached boiling point. What can I say? Do I really have to spell it out for her?

'Do I really have to spell it out for you?' I snap, aware, even as I'm speaking, that I don't even know how to spell it out for myself.

'Look, Ol, I get it, okay? You've just met your dad and it feels weird. But what did you expect? It'll take time—'

'It's not that, Charlie. Well, not just that—'

'Obviously, you feel totally weirded out. It's totally to be expected. Have you thought about speaking to one of the counsellors Ros and Mark mentioned—'

'I don't need a counsellor! Urggh! You just don't get it, do you?' I feel the heat rising and my cheeks start to burn. I don't know how to stop my voice getting louder and angrier. 'You've had a dad all your life. I've waited and waited and we went through all this… this… drama... And for what?'

Charlie folds her arms and frowns. 'I thought you were happy to have found him. I mean, isn't that what you've always wanted?'

I don't answer, so she sits down gently by my side and drapes an arm around my shoulder. 'I get it, Ol. I really do. When my dad moved out, it took me a long time to get used to seeing him on weekends by appointment. But it gets easier—'

'Stop! Don't you dare compare your dad with Alexandros!' I roar. I'm so in-her-face our noses are nearly touching. 'You've always had your dad in your life, a dad who loves you and takes care of you and is kind and thoughtful and puts you first.'

'But your dad will be all those things too,' she says smoothly, stroking my wiry hair, now let loose and bouncing around uncontrollably. Her soft, patient voice only makes me even more furious.

'What would you know?' I yell, pushing her hand away. 'You have no idea what all this is like for me. Have you even thought about my feelings? No! Because it's all about you, as usual. It's about being on a TV show. That's all you've ever cared about. Admit it, Charlie. The real reason we're here, all of it, is because you got carried away with the idea of being on the show. And then rubbing everyone's noses in it back at school when they find out you're "famous",' I sneer, waggling my fingers to make air quotes.

'Stop it, Ol. Really, I mean it. Just stop!' Charlie demands, her tone a mixture of threat and fear. The expression on her face reminds me she's never seen me lose it like this. Mum's the only one who knows just how hot my temper can be.

'No, I won't stop. And you won't be famous, anyway, Charlie. Because you're not even on the show. Because it's not all about you for a change. You're a nobody for once. I'm the star of the show. So deal with it!'

I pause to catch my breath, my heart racing. I bang my clenched fists on my thighs and then, to my horror, I start to bawl. Fat tears tumble down my cheeks to the accompaniment of horrible, ugly sobs. The last thing I want is to cry but there's no way I can stop myself, not even knowing how stupid and babyish and ugly I must look. I want to run, to get far away and leave all this behind me.

But even as the thought comes into my head I know there's no escape. This is my mess and I'm just going to have to deal with it. Alone.

Charlie kneels in front of me and holds my wrists, firmly enough to stop me hurting myself, but gently enough to calm me. I look at her and wonder what she must think of me. Have I blown it? Will we ever be friends again after all this? I think over all the mean things I said. I suppose I should apologise. But I meant them.

I sniff but the sobs are under control and Charlie passes me a box of tissues. I blow my nose noisily.

'Sorry,' I mumble.

'Don't be. You've done nothing wrong, Ol. And you're right, I did get carried away with the show and everything. I realise now how selfish I've been. I should have been supporting you more. As you said, this is all about you.'

'Don't be so nice,' I huff. 'You're going to make me cry all over again.'

'Nothing wrong with that, cry all you like, Ol. I'm totally here for you. Haven't we always been able to tell each other everything? I feel like you've closed yourself off lately. I had no idea what was going on with you.'

'Well, maybe you should have asked,' I grumble.

'Okay, okay, I'm the one who should be sorry. I realise that now. But I'm here whenever you feel ready to talk.'

'Thanks,' I shrug. There's so much I want to say

I don't know where to start.

A heavy silence fills the room. Then Charlie's phone buzzes; for once, she ignores it.

I take a deep breath, then another one, and pull my suitcase out of the wardrobe. Without a word, I unzip the case, lift out the shoebox and place it in Charlie's hands.

She looks up at me. I nod, and she slides off the lid. Her fingertips start to pick through the cards, then she pulls one out. It's the invitation to my birthday party. She reads it and slides it back in its place. The next one she pulls out is a Father's Day card. She reads the message and slips it back inside. This carries on for several minutes, with neither of us saying a word.

At last, Charlie speaks. 'Wow.'

'I never showed you these before. I was afraid you'd think they were lame,' I whisper.

I wait for my tears to well up again, but am relieved to find I'm calmer now. Must be the breathing. But then I notice Charlie's wiping her eyes with the back of her hand. I pass her the tissue box.

'Oh, Ol. I had no idea,' she sniffs. 'Are you planning on handing them over to him? Is that why you brought them with you?'

'Well, that was the plan,' I nod. 'But now I'm not so sure. There something not right about Alexandros.'

'What do you mean?' she asks, dabbing her

cheeks to check for mascara smudges.

'Call it a sixth sense or whatever. But I just don't feel anything for him. And it's not just because I haven't known him long. There's something... I dunno, secretive about him. Like he's hiding something. I know Mum feels it, too.'

Charlie sits up straight.

'I think I know what you mean,' she nods, her eyes narrowing, as she gets on her 'thinking' face. 'I mean, it was a pretty strange family reunion, right? Just a few cousins and then all that drinking and partying. He hardly spoke to you or your mum.'

'Exactly. He seemed pretty pleased with himself, like he was celebrating something. But he showed no interest at all in me.' I swallow down a lump of disappointment.

'And that mention of the grandma, my grandma, what was the word, "*yiayia*"? If I have a grandma, why wasn't she at the taverna tonight? It just doesn't add up.'

'If you have a Greek grandma, you totally need to meet her. Do you think she even knows about you? I can't believe any granny worthy of the name wouldn't want to meet her grandchild.'

'Alexandros said she did. But now I wonder about a lot of things he's said.'

'Look, Ol. If no one's going to tell us what's going on, we're going to have to find out for ourselves.'

I can see Charlie's brain is working hard by the

look of concentration on her face. *Here comes the light bulb moment.*

'I've got it!' Charlie announces. *And there it is.* Charlie kneels on the bed and sits back on her heels. 'Alexandros mentioned she lives in the next village, right? Maybe it's time to do some research of our own.'

'Um, yeah. But there are quite a few villages round here. How do we know which one she lives in?' I argue, my mind filling with lists of reasons why this won't work. For a start, it's pitch dark outside and we have no means of transport. 'We can't do anything on our own. Why don't we wait until morning and ask Mum and your dad to help,' I suggest, knowing even as the words tumble out of my mouth that Charlie is going to brush my doubts aside. When she's on a mission there's no stopping her. 'You're on a mission, aren't you?' I sigh, but I can't help the ripples of excitement making me shiver at the thought of solving this mystery at last.

'Look, Ol. The way I see it, there's nothing to lose. We, I mean *you*, have come all this way and the least you can expect is closure. To know once and for all who your dad is, what this Alexandros guy is about and to meet your Greek granny. If we don't find out now, then when? Do you really want to go home with all these unanswered questions nagging away at you?'

I shake my head and push the shoe box under

the bed with my foot.

'I still don't know what we can do tonight, though,' I point out, curious to know what my cousin is going to come up with.

'We're going to have to ask Ros,' she answers firmly, holding up a hand to quell any arguments I might make. I open my mouth and close it again, knowing there's no point. 'Now, before you even think of saying "no", it's really our only option. And think about it, she has done all the background research, well, her researchers will have. My point is, if anyone knows about your dad, if anyone has a lead that can answer all our questions, it's her.'

'Do you really think she'd help us, though?' I wonder out loud. 'I mean, all she really cares about is the show, and she's done all the filming. Didn't she say she flies home tomorrow?'

'Exactly, that's why we need to act now,' nods my cousin excitedly. 'Come on, we need to find her room number. I'll ask at reception.'

We step quietly out of the room and tiptoe along the empty corridor to the marble staircase, Charlie crouching down and peering through the handrails to check who's around in the reception and bar area, and me wondering if we're going to get into trouble for wandering around the hotel late at night when we should be in bed. Suddenly, she grabs my hand and mouths 'Shhhh!', pulling me down beside her onto the marble step. She points downwards and I lean across her to see Ros, sitting in one of the leather chairs in the foyer, with her back to us. She's talking to someone on her phone. I can only make out a few words; I hold my breath and listen harder. She's saying something about 'rights' and 'contracts' and 'pulling the plug' and at first I think it's just general business talk, but then her voice gets louder and we hear the words 'just a child' and 'morally unacceptable' and now Ros is really getting angry, and she's shouting 'Well, screw the TV Gold Award. And screw you!' She throws the mobile down and it bounces off the seat and onto the floor. Charlie turns to look at me, her mouth gaping open. My heart's racing and my brain is chasing to catch up with what just happened. We watch Ros lean down and pick up the phone, jabbing an agitated finger at the smashed screen. She stands and turns and... looks up. She sees us and we freeze.

She's clearly furious. 'What on earth are you two doing there, spying on me?' she growls, her hands on her hips. 'Well?' Charlie and I look at each other, then at Ros. I will Charlie to come up with a sensible answer that will seem both believable and innocent at the same time. But even Charlie can't spin her way out of this one.

'Get down here, you two,' she sighs. 'Where are the others? Do your parents know you're wandering about on your own?' She's calmer now, so we stand up and gingerly make our way down to the bottom of the steps. 'How much of that did you hear?' she asks, looking from one to the other. Ros does that thing that teachers do: look right into your eyes so you feel like they can read your mind and there's no point in lying.

Some instinct takes over and I realise this is the moment that I need to speak for myself, not wait for Charlie's lead. I need Ros's help. And, whether or not she is willing to give it, I have to ask. It's now or never.

'I don't think Alexandros is my real dad,' I blurt, the words tumbling out of me in my hurry to be heard and understood. 'I think you might have the answers I need. All I want is to find my dad. Can you help me find him? Please?'

Ros blinks. The barman appears behind her and starts to noisily stack glasses. 'Let's go somewhere else and talk,' Ros nods, leading us towards the lift.

'Wow!' breathes Charlie, looking out of the glass wall of Ros's penthouse suite at the twinkling lights of the village houses studding the hillside to the right. To the left, the distant beach is visible, the fishing boats in the harbour bobbing gently on shallow waves illuminated by a line of streetlamps dotted along the promenade.

'Beautiful, isn't it?' agrees Ros, sliding the glass door open. We follow her outside to the breezy balcony under the stars. 'I just love this place,' she sighs. 'Makes you think about what life should be about, you know? So beautiful…' she trails off, lost in her own thoughts.

I glance at Charlie, who pulls a 'whatever' face.

'Ros,' I venture, determined to remind her of the more pressing issues, such as *finding my father*. I stare into the distance and wonder if he's actually out there somewhere before taking a breath. 'Do you know which village my grandmother lives in? Alexandros said something about her living somewhere nearby.'

Ros turns to look at me. She leans backwards against the glass-topped table but it slides away from her along the floor tiles, making her nearly lose her balance.

She beckons us to follow her back inside. 'Let's go in and sit down. I want to show you something,' she says.

Ros's suite consists of a huge open plan area with a table in the middle (Charlie wants to know if this is where she holds all the important meetings), a door leading to a massive bedroom and adjoining bathroom (Charlie wants to know if she has a jacuzzi, to which Ros answers with a shake of her head) and another room which seems to house all Ros's suitcases (Charlie asks if this is the dressing room).

'Right, that's enough of the *tour*,' Ros insists gently, steering me towards the table. There are boxes and files and papers strewn across the shiny wooden surface. She sits on one of the swivel chairs and Charlie and I sit down on either side of her.

'This,' she indicates towards the piles of paperwork in front of us, 'is all the research I, or mostly my team, have gathered in preparation for the show. There's more stored on the computer, obviously. And they've been thorough. Believe me, these guys know what they're doing. Roger, I don't know if you've met him, is an ex-police detective. And the thing is—'

She leans back and scrapes her fingers through her short blonde hair. 'The thing is, Olivia, in spite of all our investigations, looking into your Greek family's personal history, trying to match up what we have with the official documents we could find – birth certificate, school records, tax accounts (and, trust me, I had to call in a lot of favours to get any information of use in that department), based on what your mother has told us, we simply couldn't find a trail leading to your father. It just went cold from the year he graduated and left England.'

'Hang on, Ros. Are you saying that you knew all along that Alexandros, that guy who you introduced me to on the show as my long-lost father, is not actually him at all?' Rumbles of anger are gathering somewhere under my ribs. 'Are you saying you've been lying to me all along? Just for the sake of a TV show and your precious award?'

'Ol, wait, I think Ros is trying to explain,' my cousin cuts me off gently. I'm just about to explode into a furious rant when Charlie nudges me and I see that Ros has slumped forward onto the table, her head nestled into her elbows. Is she crying?

Charlie rests her palm on Ros's back. 'Are you okay, Ros? What's wrong?' My cousin summons way more kindness than I'm feeling towards Ros. I mean, what exactly is going on here? I need to know and I need to know now.

'Ros,' I begin, my voice harsh with anguish. 'What are you saying, exactly? This whole thing has been a joke? Did you really drag me and my mum all the way here just to make some fake episode just to improve your audience ratings? Don't you have any... any...' I search my brain for the right word... *'feelings?'* My voice cracks on that final word, betraying my pain and disappointment. I bite my lip and hold in the tears, determined not to let her humiliate me any further, if that's even possible.

Ros lifts her head up and faces me. Her eyes look tired and all her energy seems to have leaked away somehow. 'You're right, sweetheart. And you're right to be angry. It's all... all a complete mess!' She grabs handfuls of her hair and shakes her head from side to side in despair.

My cousin interrupts Ros's impending meltdown. 'Hang on, Ros, if this is a mess, *you* need to sort it out. There's no good just having a hissy fit. We've come this far – tell us what you know and we'll come up with a plan. Together.'

Ros slumps down in her seat and looks at Charlie through bleary eyes.

'You don't understand. How could you, you're just kids. It's not that simple. Don't you think if there was a way to sort this out, to find what happened to Olivia's father, we would have worked it out by now? And anyway—'

'Hold on a minute,' my cousin protests, holding up a hand and actually stopping Ros mid-sentence. 'Let's just remember a few things here.' Got to hand it to my cousin – she's doing a great job of taking control. I can't wait to hear what she's going to say next. 'First, it was my idea, mine and Ol's, to write to your show and it's because of us that we're all here in the first place. We trusted you, because that's what your show is supposed to be about, reuniting families that have lost touch, right?'

Obediently, Ros nods her head in agreement. Charlie is amazing when she's on a roll.

'So, you need to keep to your side of the bargain. And second,' her eyes dart across to meet mine for a second, 'we're here now, in Greece. We must be so close. How can you expect us to just walk away and leave things as they are? More to the point, how can you, an award-winning TV programme maker, pack up and go home knowing that there's a mystery to be solved right here, and that we're so close to finding out the truth?'

'Not to mention the contract,' I add, a note of warning creeping into my tone. Charlie does a tiny tilt of her head as a signal to let her do the talking. I take the hint – I trust her to do what's right for me.

145

I guess I always have, in spite of our recent arguments.

Ros looks from Charlie to me then back at Charlie and I sense something shift in her mind. She even sits up a bit straighter and starts to shuffle through some of the papers.

'Let's start with the birth certificate. Your father was baptised in a church in the village of Paramithi.'

'Yes, yes!' I allow myself a moment of excitement as hope starts to build again, even after so many disappointments. 'I remember now. That's the village my mum mentioned ages ago when we first started talking about finding my… you know, *him*. Mark gave me a picture.'

'Have you been there to talk to anyone who might have known him?' Charlie asks Ros, shaking her head and mouthing 'doh' as Ros explains that when Alexandros came forward and presented himself, they didn't do too much more digging and took his word for it that he was my dad.

'So, he could be anybody, any old stranger comes along and says they're the person you're looking for and, what? You just shrug your shoulders and say, 'Yeah, he'll do? This is people's lives you're dealing with here, Ros!'

'No, no. You don't understand. Alexandros, he was baptised in that church. We checked. He said he'd been to Leeds University and even showed us his Degree certificate and pictures of the graduation, celebrating with friends. Including your mum.'

'Mmm, but maybe he got hold of them somehow…'

'There were other things that he told us, lots of things that convinced us he was your dad, Olivia. And yet…'

We sit in silence waiting for more, anything, that will shed some light.

'And yet, there were some, what we might call, red flags. Like he was *very* interested in what his fee would be for the show. Normally, long-lost family members don't ask much about that side of things. Well, not until we start to talk about contracts and suchlike. And there was something Mark said, too…'

'Mark knew there were red flags but said nothing?' I gasp. I had really trusted Mark; out of everyone I'd met from the show's team, he seemed the most genuine. I winced when I remembered all he'd said about protecting me and supporting me on my journey. He even told me about finding his own father. Had he actually been lying all along? I felt sick with disappointment.

'He told *me*, but taken on balance, we felt that Alexandros's story and the evidence he showed us was enough… anyway, it was up to your mum to shout if the guy we presented her with was not her guy. I mean, really, this is not just on me. What on earth was your mum thinking? Wouldn't she recognise the father of her only child?'

I bite back my angry tears. There's no way Ros is getting away with putting the blame for this on Mum.

Charlie steers the conversation back to the pile of documents in front of us.

'Well, I say we should head to the village. What if we can find Ol's grandmother? Wouldn't she be able to offer some explanation as to what's going on here?'

'If she really is my grandmother, and this is not just another one of Alexandros's lies,' I shrug moodily.

'Well, I don't see what we've got to lose,' agrees Ros. 'The village, Paramithi, it's the next one along the coast. I went there for lunch with some of the team yesterday after filming. Gorgeous little place. We can go and visit the church, too. Someone must know something.'

'Let's just hope we find someone willing to tell us the truth,' Charlie nods. 'I mean, are all those other Alexes really his cousins? And if they are, why would they all go along with this lie?'

Ros shakes her head. 'I don't know. But I'm more determined than ever now to find some answers.' She turns to me and reaches out, placing her hands on my shoulders. 'I'm so sorry, Olivia. I really never meant it to all get so messy. But let me try to put it right, okay?'

'You mean even if you have to scrap the award-winning episode of the series?' I ask, still full of suspicion. I find it hard to believe she's going to put me before her career.

'Yes, that's exactly what I mean,' Ros sighs wearily. 'I wouldn't be able to live with knowing I'd left things as they are. It wouldn't be fair.'

I'm almost satisfied she means it, but remind myself that doing is more powerful than talking and there's a long way to go if I'm to be totally convinced.

'So, what are we waiting for?' Charlie pipes up. 'It's only ten o'clock. Early for Greece. Let's go now! Got your car keys, Ros?'

Before Ros can change her mind, Charlie scoops up some photographs and papers and sticks them in a plastic folder before leading the way out.

CHAPTER TWENTY-SIX

'This is definitely the right house; the guy in the shop said it was the one with the blue shutters and the flowers outside,' Ros says doubtfully, pulling up under a tree outside the front door of a whitewashed cottage. All the lights seem to be off, though, and the place appears to be empty. We step out of the car and Ros knocks firmly on the wooden door. Charlie's peering through one of the windows when a voice behind us makes us jump.

'Can I help you?' A woman in a smart flowery dress, her grey hair tied in a neat bun and her arms full with a stack of brown boxes, is walking towards us looking less than pleased. Not surprising, really, considering we are three strangers noseying around her house.

'Ah, you speak English. That's good,' says Ros, relieved, putting out her hand to shake. The old lady looks down at her laden arms and Ros apologises. 'Oh, sorry, of course. Can we help you with those?'

'It's all right,' she replies calmly, 'and I think the

question is how can I help you, as I ask before?'

She is cool and in control, her Greek accent strong but her words plain and simple. My heart does a fluttery thing – could this be my grandmother?

'Ah, well, it's a bit of a long story, actually,' Ros starts to explain a little breathlessly. 'Um, could we please talk to you? Elpida, is that your name? If you wouldn't mind? It's about your son, Alexandros. We are looking for him?'

The lady nods and seems to be thinking over what Ros had said. 'How you know my son?' she asks at last. I look at Charlie, wondering where to start. Charlie rummages in the folder, peering closely at the photographs in the semi-darkness. She hands one to the lady, who takes it and holds it up close to her face. 'Where did you get this picture?' she wants to know, and her tone sounds defensive. Is she going to get annoyed and tell us to go away?

'I work for a television company. We've been making a show. It's about helping people to find their lost family members…'

'Ahhh, I see,' Elpida replies calmly 'You'd better come inside. Then we can talk more.'

She pulls a key from her dress pocket, managing to balance the load in her arms at the same time as turning the key. Inside, she flicks on the light with her elbow and lets the boxes fall onto the table.

They're full of candles. Long, thin, brown-coloured candles. Not like any candles I've ever seen before. I must have been staring at them.

'These are from the monastery. They make them there, from the beeswax, and I help to sell them. It brings in a little money,' she explains patiently, looking at me properly under the bright light of the overhead bulb. My eyes are drawn to more pictures along her mantelpiece above the little fireplace, many of them featuring a young boy who looks exactly like the one in the picture she's now holding between her fingers. There's one of the same boy as a teenager, lying on the front of a speedboat in some cool sunglasses, and another one where he's wearing one of those square caps they wear at graduation. I look over at Charlie and Ros and I just know they're thinking the same as me. The guy in the pictures is not the man I met today. He looks similar, yes, there is definitely a resemblance, but no, clearly they are two different people.

I pick up the graduation photo. 'Is this your son?' I ask, hoping she doesn't tell me off for touching her personal things. Instead, she walks over to me and gently takes the photo from my hands.

'Yes, this is my Alexandros,' she whispers, before laying her palm on my shoulder. 'And this is a picture of me, when I was a young girl, about your age,' she adds, pulling another picture out of the shadows.

My hand flies to my mouth when I see what

Elpida looked like. She looks exactly like me! Same wild, curly hair, same dark eyes, same 'so what?' expression Mum always complains about when I refuse to say 'cheese' for the camera.

Ros looks over my shoulder and gasps and Charlie takes the graduation picture out of my hands.

There's a moment of silence as we each take in the information in front of us and try to make sense of the events of the last couple of days.

Before anyone can speak, an urgent knocking at the door makes all four of us jump. Elpida goes to answer it. Mum, Uncle Joe and Gran are all outside, and Mum's eyes are wild when she catches sight of us.

For a second, nobody speaks, then everybody's talking at once. And loudly.

'What on earth are you doing here?' Mum accuses, looking from me to Charlie and back again. 'Ros – please tell me what's going on here?' Before she can answer, Uncle Joe is waving his arms around and asking why we're not back at the hotel where Auntie Tash and Bernard left us and don't we know it's way past our bedtimes, which sounds so funny because clearly he's lost for words and has gone into 'confused parent' mode, which makes Charlie giggle. As if bedtimes matter when there's so much drama going on! And Gran's voice can be heard babbling over the top of Uncle Joe's and Mum's and she's saying something about needing to talk to me about my father and at the sound of that word, it all goes quiet. Ros looks at Elpida, who has been standing like a statue, watching this scene with her mouth slightly open. There's a deep sadness in her eyes and she holds the picture of her son to her chest and crosses her thin, leathery arms over each other.

'Um, Elpida,' Ros says softly. 'Is it all right if I call you that?' Elpida stays motionless, staring at the front door and avoiding our eyes. 'Can I ask you something?'

The door bursts open, snatching away the silent moment and making everyone jump. There's a tall man standing there, with large cardboard boxes under his arm (more candles, I'm guessing) and I instantly know who he is. He's Elpida's son, the man in the photograph she's still got pressed tightly to her chest. My heart starts beating wildly and I hold my breath. He drops the boxes onto the wooden floor.

His eyes register surprise at finding a crowd of strange people in his mother's cottage but he keeps his cool and walks slowly over to his mother, one of his legs dragging a little behind, making his movements slightly uneven. *'Ti yinete, mama?'* he asks her softly. His mother nods and gestures to the table. *'Ela, agape mou.* Sit down, my son. I think we need to have a long talk.'

For the first time, Alexandros's eyes rest on my mother and he takes a sharp breath.

'What... Emily? It is really you?'

'So, is this the famous Alex, then?' Gran pipes up, breaking the spell of silence hovering over the room. 'The real one, I mean?'

'Mum – how did you know...?' Mum turns to Gran, shock and confusion registering in her face.

'It was obvious, love, to me at least. That guy was not your ex, no way. There was no... what do you young people call it... *chemistry* between you two. I knew something was wrong. So I went and had a chat with the owners of that lovely taverna where we had dinner tonight, Demi and Themi, such a lovely couple. And I found out a few things about that guy, the other Alex. And, well, let's just say, it confirmed my suspicions.'

'But why would someone pretend – just to be on a TV show? That's a terrible kind of lie to tell. What sort of a man would do that?'

'People do terrible things when they are desperate,' replied Elpida, shaking her head sadly and sinking into a chair. 'When my nephew came to me asking for pictures of my son, I had no idea what he was up to. Then, with all the talk in the village about the filming, and the TV show, I started to wonder...'

'Wait, you knew about this... this deception?' Ros accuses angrily. 'How could you go along with this, knowing that it would cause so much hurt? There is a child involved. Don't you have any feelings, at all?' Charlie grips my hand and I try to make myself breathe slowly and stay calm.

Elpida puts down the picture and buries her head in her hands. 'I'm sorry,' she mumbles.

'Sorry?' Uncle Joe repeats icily. 'Look at this young girl, Elpida. Look at her. This is your granddaughter.

'I didn't know. He warned me not to speak to anyone if they asked me questions.'

Alexandros flashes a look of disbelief at his mother, but then his gaze rests on me. There's a light in his eyes and an expression of joy crosses his face. 'Wait, Emily, can you explain, before I go completely crazy? Is this beautiful girl who I think she is?'

'Yes,' smiles Mum, looking exhausted but relieved to have finally got everything in the open. 'This is our daughter, Olivia.'

I walk over to Alexandros, my dad. He puts out his arms and I step into them, letting him hug me close, and it feels so natural. Elpida gets up and joins us, her arms reaching across my dad and me. My dad. *My* dad. My *dad*.

'I am so sorry,' she says softly. 'I did not want to hurt anybody or deceive anybody.'

'But I still don't understand why you didn't tell me about this, Mama,' my dad says, shaking his head in disbelief. 'Why would you keep this from me?'

My grandmother sighs sadly. 'I didn't know there was a child involved. You have been through so much, *yie mou*. And to be honest, I didn't believe your cousin. I thought he had made up this story to get his grandfather's land. You have chosen a new path at the monastery. I thought it was better to forget the past.'

'Monastery, you say?' chips in Gran, delightedly. 'A priest in the family?' She places her palms together, looks heavenwards and crosses herself. 'I knew you had a plan,' she whispers gratefully.

'Wait, *what?*' Mum's eyes are on stalks. Ros keeps quiet, but I can tell her mind is whirring. Would this explain why my dad was so difficult to find? Was he living in some remote Greek monastery? *Is my dad a monk?*

My dad lays a hand gently on her arm. 'Let me explain,' he soothes. 'It's a long story.'

CHAPTER TWENTY-SEVEN

Charlie lays down gracefully on the sun-lounger and adjusts her headphones. I flop down on the one next to her, nearly tipping it up, my dripping hair accidentally splashing her with cold water.

'Hey!' she squeals, 'watch it!' She dabs at a tiny drop of water with her towel, then moves her phone to her other side, out of harm's way.

'Sorry,' I gasp, still catching my breath. 'I got all the way out to the blue fishing boat this time. The water's so clear, you can see all these little fish.'

'That's great, Ol, but this is my, I mean *our*, last day and I just want to make the most of the sunshine.' My cousin's tone is close to whiney; she always gets like this when she's feeling upset, and I know she's sad that we're going to be going home tomorrow.

'Yeah, but just think. We'll be able to come back to Greece soon. We can come whenever we want. We've got family here. There's my dad, my *yiayia*, my uncles…'

Charlie cuts me off: '*You'll* be able to come back

whenever you want. They're your family, Ol, not mine. They won't want me hanging around.' Charlie's in danger of entering the sulking stage of her ever-evolving mood spectrum.

'Look I know it feels like things have changed, Charlie, and they're my family, yes. But you're my family too,' I soothe, turning onto my side to face her. 'And you've always been there for me.' It makes a change for me to be the one doing the reassuring. And it occurs to me that, just as Charlie's parents have parted ways, mine have got back together.

I look down the beach to where Auntie Tash and Bernard are splashing about in the shallows, my auntie playfully starting a water fight while Bernard pretends he doesn't mind having water thrown in his face. He's got so much sun cream on, he looks like an oven-ready chicken. 'I can't believe they went skinning-dipping last night. I bet it was your mum's idea,' I remark. 'Poor Bernard. Do you think your mum's serious about him? They seem pretty loved up.'

'Uggh! *Gross*. Don't make me think about that, *please*, Ol. It's bad enough we've had to see so much of his hairy flesh this week. I can't deal with the whole "new phase of the relationship" stuff. And I prefer not to think about my mum getting serious with her boyfriend. If you don't mind!'

I lay back on the sun lounger and close my eyes. I feel sorry that my cousin's not having a great time at the moment and remind myself that she is still upset about her mum and dad breaking up. It's just that I can't help feeling more excited and happy than I remember feeling, ever. I've found my dad. He loves me. I even think he and Mum might pick up where they left off, though Gran warned me not to expect any fairy tale endings. It's enough that I know where he is. I'm not expecting miracles.

This morning, I gave him the box with all my letters and cards to him. He read every single one and Mum had to keep passing him the tissue box, he cried so much as he read them.

We'd had breakfast together at the hotel. Sitting between my mum and dad, chatting about our plans for the future, almost made up for all the birthdays and Christmases we'd missed out on.

When Alex and Mark had appeared, much the worse for wear after a long night that ended up in the local nightclub (again), to order black coffees and sit out on the terrace to nurse their hangovers behind dark glasses, Gran was the only one who could bring herself to talk to them. She'd gone over for one of her little chats, and reported later that she'd given them both a piece of her mind.

'I told your fake Dad, Alex, and his new friend, Mark, that there's nothing wrong with being gay. They should get out of the closet, isn't that what they say, mmm? But pretending to be someone you're not, well, that's just wrong. Didn't he realise how this hurts people? And he can't use being gay as an excuse. There's nothing wrong with that. Sure that Elton John fella does fantastic charity work.'

While Charlie and I exchanged open-mouthed stares and took in this new and unknown gay-friendly side of Gran, Dad filled us in on what might have made his cousin take part in this ludicrous lie.

'It is difficult here, to be gay is to be different. It is not always approved of. Family, fatherhood, that is the important thing for a man here. Many families would prefer to pretend no one is gay, especially not one of their own sons. They would prefer to live a lie than accept it. Maybe my cousin thought having a daughter would bring him respect.'

'Well, there are some very judgemental people around, that's for sure,' Gran had nodded, and told us she'd promised to pray for Alex. 'Apparently, he's talking about going back to England with Mark, seeing if he can find an easier way to live his life in his own way.'

'Did you see Ros this morning, before she left?' Mum had asked. Charlie and I had shaken our heads; we'd slept in after all the excitement of last night. 'Well, she wants to set up a meeting with us when we get back,' Mum had informed me. Even before I had finished rolling my eyes, Mum had gone on to explain that the show was going to be dropped but we would still receive our fee. 'What about the TV Awards?' Charlie had quizzed her, wondering perhaps if she was going to miss out on a red carpet event. 'Ros is giving up reality TV,' Mum had said. 'She said she'd always wanted to get into making documentaries and this had given her an idea. She wants to make a film about what goes on behind the scenes on reality shows. To "explore the human cost of all this personal drama being played out for mass entertainment", was the phrase she used, I believe.' Mum paused and leaned in. 'Olivia, she's asked if we would like to take part in her film, but of course it is totally up to you.'

'Oh, Ol…' Charlie begins but a glare from me silences her. She's squirming in her chair and biting her lip with the effort of keeping her suggestion to herself.

'I'll think about it,' I promise. But I have to put the idea out of my mind for now. There's been enough drama. I look from my mum's face to my dad's and back again, still trying to take it all in and believe this is really happening. Dad winks at me and gives me a little nod. I know he gets me.

He and Mum talked for hours last night, alone. They'd found a quiet spot under the olive trees behind his mother's house and sat together, filling in the blanks of the last fourteen years.

It turns out, Alexandros had had to return to Greece after their graduation, to have treatment for cancer. He'd decided not to tell my mum because he wanted to have happy memories of their time together. Also, he didn't know if he would recover. He'd had chemotherapy and radiotherapy, and the cancer had gone, but the doctors explained that one of the side effects was that he would never be able to be a father. He knew Mum wanted children and that he could never offer her the kind of life she – or any woman – would wish for. So he'd decided to close that chapter of his life. And he'd heard from their friend, Rob, that Mum had settled down and had a family. (Mum was furious when she heard that. She said she'd only told Rob that because he kept asking her out.) He'd given up his flat in Athens and moved back to the village to live with his parents after his treatment, which explained why he'd never received Mum's letters. Then, he'd fallen into a deep depression. He'd taken to drinking. One night, he was walking back from the village bar and had been hit by a car. His leg had been trapped under the twisted metal. He couldn't even remember what had happened, but he knew he'd been drinking too much. He'd lost so much blood he had to have several blood transfusions. For a week, he was in a coma. When he finally woke up, he knew he had to make some big changes in his life. If he couldn't be a father, or have a family, he would instead try to help others who had struggled as he had with life's challenges.

His leg was severely damaged, but at least he could walk. He'd found a job at the nearby monastery, helping keep the bees and look after the kitchen garden. Most of the monks were old and needed someone around to help them out. He had thought about taking his vows one day, but he had plans to build a house of welcome, a retreat, a quiet place of reflection where people could come and stay, when life was too much. There was a piece of land behind his mother's house that would be the perfect spot. He just had to find a way to get a bank loan; it was difficult with his tiny income.

Mum had told me all of this the next day, after Ros, Charlie, Gran, Uncle Joe and I had said our goodbyes to Elpida and been told to get some much-needed sleep. Not that I had slept much that night, obviously. Charlie and I had sat up till dawn, talking about the events of the most dramatic couple of days ever.

Mum had taken my hand in hers and we'd walked down to the little harbour just after breakfast. Sitting on the edge of the jetty, watching the little boats tapping against the harbour wall, she'd explained the whole story to me. I wanted to know how she felt about him, of course, if they were still in love, but I knew it wasn't the time to ask. For now, I'd found my dad. And that was more than enough. That was my miracle.

CHAPTER TWENTY-EIGHT

'Oh, it's just like in the film, *Mamma Mia!*' gasps Gran, like an excited teenager. I couldn't remember ever seeing her so full of joy.

We're following my dad up the steep stony pathway to the little church at the top of the hill. The sun is setting just behind the slope, bathing the rocks in an orange-pink glow. Everyone is here, wearing their smartest clothes: Charlie, Gran, Mum and Dad, Auntie Tash and Bernard, and Uncle Joe with Maria from the guest house.

'If you think about it, it's more like *Mamma Mia* backwards,' points out Charlie, pausing to pout at her phone for a selfie.

'What, "*Aim Ammam*"?' asks Bernard, clearly confused. He stops to shake dry earth and tiny stones out of his shiny black loafers.

'Noooo,' Charlie shakes her head and rolls her eyes.

'Oh, I see what you mean,' Gran nods, stopping to catch her breath and wiping beads of sweat from her forehead with the back of her hand. 'Olivia has travelled to Greece to find her father, instead of her father travelling to Greece to find his daughter.'

'Exactly, Gran. *Thank you!*' Charlie leans in to Gran for a joint photo and Gran puts her hand on her hip and strikes a pose. 'Suck in your cheeks, Gran, it shows your bone structure.' Gran pouts obediently and Mum hides her giggles behind a discreet cough.

'I have heard of this film but I have never seen it,' my dad smiles. 'Perhaps I should now.'

'Can we watch it together?' I ask, imagining the three of us sitting cosily on our sofa back home. Dad puts his arm round my shoulder and gives me a squeeze. We still haven't sorted out when he's going to come and visit us but there's no harm in planting the idea in his head. 'Don't worry, now I've found you I'm going to make sure I make up for all those years I missed being your dad,' he smiles, apparently reading my mind.

Finally, we're at the top of the hill, in front of the little church.

'Ready?' he asks me and I nod.

Dad takes my hand and Mum's, and we walk together into the tiny church. It's like a cave inside; the walls are rough, and pictures of saints, all reds and gold, glow in the flickering candle light. There are chairs set out in rows with various family members sitting ready and waiting – the young Alexes wave in our direction, and there are some of my dad's aunts and uncles I recognise from the photos. Elpida stands up to greet us. '*Yiassou,*

Yiayia,' I say shyly, trying to get used to the new phrases I've been learning.

We take our places in front of the altar and the others shuffle into their seats behind us. A priest in a long black robe stands with his back to us. He starts to chant and make crosses in the air with his arm. Then he turns and starts to speak in Greek.

When he's finished, my dad turns to the assembled guests and Mum and I turn around too, while he translates.

'Welcome everybody, family and friends, new and old. Thank you for coming to share this special day. As you know, I recently found out that I have a daughter. This beautiful young lady, Olivia. When I fell in love with her mother, Emily, all those years ago, we had talked about having children and I explained that the first daughter is always named after her grandmother. It is our Greek tradition. Elpida, please can you come forward?'

Elpida stands and walks up to us, her best shoes tapping on the stone tiles.

Elpida means 'Hope' and today we have come to baptise my daughter with her spiritual name.'

We turn back towards the altar and the priest begins to chant again. I tip my head forward over a marble basin when he lifts a handful of cool water and it slips through his fingers and onto my hair. I don't follow what he's saying but I hear the name 'Elpida'.

A few minutes later the ceremony is over.

There are hugs and kisses and gifts in small boxes and envelopes pressed into my hands.

As we step out into the dusk, there's a shuffling and everyone turns to see Bernard down on one knee, looking up at Auntie Tash and holding out a small open box.

Charlie claps a hand to her forehead and groans. 'No way! You're not going to do this *now* are you?'

'Absolutely, I am,' Bernard grins, squinting up at my auntie. Charlie puts her fingers in her ears and squeezes her eyes shut.

'Ugh, *such* a cliché,' mutters my cousin, while the smiling crowd applauds.

CHAPTER TWENTY-NINE

'Hold this,' Dad says, passing me the end of a measuring tape. He paces backwards, feeding out the tape as he goes, letting it fall flat on the dry earth. When he reaches the last of the olive trees in the row, he stops and looks at the number on the tape, pulls a pen from behind his ear and scribbles the measurement down in his notebook.

'Mmmm, just as I thought. We could build up to here, with enough room for a courtyard in the middle.'

'And maybe a pool?' suggests Charlie hopefully.

'We'll see,' Dad answers, smiling.

'We want it to be a sustainable, eco-friendly place, Charlie,' Uncle Joe points out.

It turned out it was true that my great-grandfather had promised some land to the first of his grandsons to have a child. Because of me, my dad had inherited this piece of land and he was finally able to start building.

Charlie's dad is taking pictures and sketching out the floorplan of the building on a large pad of paper. He's offered to stay and help with the building work, says he's always wanted a project like this to throw himself into. Charlie thinks it's more likely that it's Maria's arms her dad is really keen to throw himself into, but hey, as she pointed out, if it means she can come and visit then she's not going to argue.

'How long do you think it will take?' I ask, walking over and helping roll up the tape.

Dad looks into the distance and considers this question. I love how he takes all my questions so seriously. We've talked at great length about the retreat and he listened to all my suggestions, like having a wall of glass where visitors could watch the sunset and a shaded area for yoga sessions and a quiet place under the lemon trees for meditation. He seemed really impressed with my ideas; I didn't want to tell him Charlie and I had Googled retreats around the world for ideas. Some had full-on spa treatments and five-star accommodation, complete with top chefs and excursions to nearby landmarks, to keep the visitors entertained. I knew Dad wanted something more simple, relaxing and peaceful. It would be a retreat in the spiritual sense, 'a quiet place to heal and escape the pressures of modern life' it said on the website he'd started to put together. I couldn't see a swimming pool being part of the authentic Greek village experience. Besides, the sea was just at the bottom of the hill, a short walk away.

'I think we might be able to start to welcome our

first guests by next spring,' he replies, pinching a leaf from one of the trees and squeezing it between his finger and thumb. He holds it under my nose and raises an eyebrow.

I sniff in the scent; it's vaguely medicinal, reminding me of the little bottles of oil Gran sometimes sniffs when she's got a cold. 'Eucalyptus?' I offer in reply to his unspoken question.

He nods, impressed at how much I've already learnt about the outdoor life here in a short time: the names of some of the insects, a few of the shrubs and plants. Charlie is not impressed and keeps calling me 'Nature Girl' but I don't think that's a bad thing to be, so I'm not offended.

'And these are olives, aren't they?' I ask, pointing at the row of trees standing to attention on the border of the field.

'These are your family trees,' jokes Mum. I know she's thinking back to the day when I was supposed to research my own 'family tree' for Mr Lemone's History homework. I swallow, remembering how upset I was, how much I hated not knowing who my dad was, who *I* was, and let the ripples of joy I feel every time I look at him, at my dad, remind me how lucky I am to have finally found him.

Acknowledgements

First, a huge thanks to publisher Shaun Russell for his creative energy and enthusiasm for storytelling, and to all the team at Candy Jar Books, especially editor Keren Williams. Special thank you to Martin Baines and Kath Northam for the cover design.

Thanks also to the staff on the MA Children's Literature course at Goldsmiths, University of London, especially Professor Michael Rosen, Doctor Julia Hope and Doctor Maggie Pitfield, for sharing their passion for the academic study of children's books and teaching me to *problematise*. The idea for this novel took shape in a creative writing workshop, and I am sincerely grateful to my peers and to my tutors, Ardu Vakil, Sara Grant and Jenny Downham for their encouragement and critical guidance.

A big thank you to Jon Appleton for his professional advice and to Brian Moses for the kind words and helpful suggestions.

Thanks to Michelle for all the patience, kindness and support (and for the pomegranate margaritas) and to Marie, for making the adventurous look easy and reminding me to stretch.

To my book group comrades, past and present – thank you for the company, good humour and insights.

To my family, immediate and extended, Irish and Greek, nearby and far flung.

And finally, thanks to Elise, Anton and John, for encouraging me, reminding me of my deadlines and providing many, many cups of tea.